UNDER THE STREETS OF L.A.

A yellow-orange gas was belching out of the manhole in thick puffs, and in the middle of it a hand reached up, and a voice was gasping something.

The DPW men grabbed the hand. "What the . . . Carlos! What the hell?" They yanked him up, and he collapsed to the pavement, twitching, barely breathing.

"Get an ambulance!" Del screamed at the cop, who was already running to her car.

They carefully turned Carlos over. His face was scorched black. Clothes were melted to his body. "Jesus Christ!" Chuck whispered.

"Carlos!" Del said, leaning his face close to the injured man, disregarding the ugliness and stink. "What the hell happened down there? Can you talk? Can you hear me?"

He tried to speak, but blood gurgled up instead.

Del cradled his head. "What about the other guys?" he asked.

Carlos began to move his mouth. "They're gone," he rasped. "So hot . . . burned . . . I couldn't . . ."

His head lolled to one side.

VOLCANO

Story by Jerome Armstrong
Screenplay by Jerome Armstrong and Billy Ray
Directed by Mick Jackson
Novelization by Richard Woodley

HarperPaperbacks
A Division of HarperCollinsPublishers

HarperPaperbacks
A Division of HarperCollinsPublishers
10 East 53rd Street, New York, N.Y. 10022-5299

ISBN 0-06-101165-7

HarperCollins®, ®, and HarperPaperbacks™ are trademarks of HarperCollinsPublishers Inc.

First printing: May 1997

Printed in the United States of America

Visit HarperPaperbacks on the World Wide Web at
http://www.harpercollins.com/paperbacks

❖ 10 9 8 7 6 5 4 3 2 1

VOLCANO

1
RUMBLE

Geology should have been over a couple of minutes ago, but, as usual, the class picked up at the end, when Professor Heim got cute.

"We believe that the core may be turning at a slightly faster rate than the earth itself," he said, narrowing his eyes as if peering into a dark distance instead of the rear wall.

"What do you mean 'may'?" asked a junior with a ring in his eyebrow, as the students began to gather up their books.

"I mean, it may be turning at a rate that gives it an entire extra revolution—one more lap than we get—in a hundred years. We're talking about a hunk of iron under so much pressure that at seven thousand degrees it's still a solid hunk, fifteen hundred miles across—a little smaller than the moon; here to Kansas City, say—that is moving rather independently from the rest of the earth. Spinning on its own, so to speak. If in fact we know what we're talking about."

Now the lean professor widened his eyes devilishly. It was track season—it was almost always track season in this climate—at Long Beach State, and his thoughts ran back to those wonderful agonies of fifteen hundred meters in the smoggy sun and the brutal two-hundred-meter reps that gave him stamina, back when he had stamina, back when the air was better, his breathing was better, and tanned, leggy lovelies such as those who sat before him and to whom he now preached densities, heat, and earth shivers were available to him and he could go forever.

"What do you mean, 'if'?"

"What I mean is, if the core is turning at a faster rate than the rest of the earth, at such a heat and mass—and that's what we think, from our seismic instruments and computer models and all that jazz that a couple of days or decades from now could seem as primitive as an oxcart—if that's true, what about it? What I want you to think about is, what would such a variance produce in tectonic movement and magma pressures? That is, what is going on in the earth? Take a shot. Your guess is as good as mine. Next time."

As the students shuffled out the door, he turned

and erased the blackboard on which he had drawn a crude cross section of the earth, on which he had labeled the center section, "core, approx 1,500 miles diameter (1% of earth's volume), 7,000 degrees," and a way out from that a huge inverted teardrop plume of magma, which he labeled "40,000 feet tall," rising through the earth's innards "4,000 miles" down, like a helium balloon soaring through a gaudy, striated heaven, with question marks all over the place above it. To him, it was all about the evils of mortality, the futility and vanity of humankind. But it would be years before any of these kids would know what the hell he was talking about if he told them what he was really thinking.

Sun Dip hadn't always believed, but he believed now, because of the car. The rusting hulk of a green-and-white '57 Chevy Bel Air had been left where somebody evidently had gotten it stuck after wandering off Route 15 for a little drunken off-roading and let its wheels slip over the edge of a dry wash, where it had hung for years, gradually stripped of its usable electrical parts by ATV nomads. Until lately, when it began to sink, and then the whole immediate area around it began to sink in the sand, so that the car was mysteriously disappearing into a deepening cup the size of the Hollywood Bowl.

That was mystery enough for Sun Dip. He had watched the process over recent weeks as the wheels disappeared, then the fenders and fins. It was inexorable, and inexorability to him suggested immortality, or the need at least to address the issue right away. The earth and earthliness were swallowing us up. The car was a chariot in which his handful of disciples would ride to eternity, or at least be transported in rapture until the buzz wore off. There was a definite buzz produced down in that declivity, in that car, and it was better, more convincing, than peyote or grass, because he didn't have to give them anything. They yielded up to him their earthly possessions. To him it was all free.

"Om," intoned Sun Dip.

"Om, oooooom," answered the three women and two men sitting cross-legged in their saffron robes in a hunched circle amid the sagebrush awash in dawn sun, their hands resting on the toes of their Tevas, with thumbs touching forefingers a lace fringe of digital loops.

Sun Dip had been a good deal more cynical when he began this mission three years ago, when he was still just insurance agent Marc Rosenbaum, when he was twenty pounds heavier and had more hair, when he decided that mystical power was the way to go, and all you needed was a handful of rich kids with hot hormones and you could have everything you wanted by the time you were thirty. Which was good, because he could see he would be bald by the time he was forty. But these hours out in the Mojave had changed him. He had begun to feel the buzz. Maybe he was really called. Maybe he really did know how to save souls, or at least where you went to get them saved. When the earth had started to change around this spot a month ago, and the car started to sink, he began to get the buzz and have visions. Now he actually believed that the world was coming to an end and he had found the safety chute.

Now he rose, eyes almost closed, and they rose with him. He led the oming procession down into the grand declivity, churning the loosened sand, to the Chevy, where he gestured majestically to the rolled-down windows, which were by now at ground level. One by one they slithered in, mindless of the dirt on their saffron robes, or the small rips that entered the seams.

They squeezed together in the early chill on the sunken seats, bowed their heads, and welcomed the buzz. Which in this case was final.

Sheriff Strock recovered them after his deputy had found them pursuant to some calls from concerned parents who suggested a desert search because they knew about Sun Dip. The sheriff himself had become curiously light-headed in the effort, and he mentioned that fact to the pathologist, who came up with the notion of carbon dioxide, a presence confirmed by the visit of an L.A. forensics team to the site.

"Sometimes it just comes up out of the earth like an odorless belch," the pathologist said, "and because it's heavier than air, it just lies there, like what they found up at Mammoth Lake a few years ago, knocking off prairie dogs and scorpions and anything else that wanders into it, until the belching stops and eventually it just dissipates and goes away and nobody ever knows anything."

"These kids were just unlucky, then," mused the sheriff, nodding, "that this cloud of stuff was sitting there."

"Might not happen again for a million years," the pathologist said. "Or San Francisco might go to sleep tomorrow."

"That was a 6.2 quake yesterday, someplace out there, epicenter the Four Corners area, they think."

"What else is new? They've had shudders lately in New England, and everybody in Vermont goes nuts and hollers about atomic testing, which hasn't happened in ten years and isn't the problem anyway. Nothing's the problem. How the hell they think they got *their* mountains?"

"The planet is a living thing," the sheriff offered thoughtfully.

"Well, more so than those five kids and Sun Dip."

A FEW DAYS EARLIER. . .
The air was foul at Third and La Cienega, and so

was the mood in the otherwise bright hour of 9:00
A.M. Police had cordoned off the entire block of
Third Street between La Cienega and San Vicente
Boulevards, where a proposed subway stop was to
be built, with metal barricades, and outside the barricades were two growing knots of grumpy
protesters from the neighborhood and area, one
group of largely upscale whites dressed in casual
pastels opposing the stop, the other group, composed more of Hispanics and blacks dressed in
more assertive colors, opposing the opposers. Some
of those opposing the construction were holding up
signs saying, "S.T.O.P. Sensible Transit Only,
Please," and, "Not here!" and "What About Our
Children?" The other side held placards reading,
"P.E.T. People for Equality in Transit," and "We
Need to Ride Too," and, in ironic echo, "What
About Our Children?"

Behind the barricades, where cops stood with
legs apart and arms folded across their chests, chat-
ting among themselves while keeping an eye on the
groups, was planted a single innocuous metal sign
bearing the slogan, "We Move Ahead of the
Problems—L.A. Metro Transit Authority."

TV trucks had been there first, of course, cameras setting up just after dawn, and they were
ready when the first of the groups drifted in. But
their first real moment was now, when two indi-
viduals emerged from their respective groups to
stand face-to-face and bark at each other, with

distinctive clarity, in the very shadow of the shops and restaurants and movie theaters within the hulking monolith of two hundred establishments that is the Beverly Center.

The young woman wearing a large button proclaiming: "Lydia Perez—Chicana Pride!" confronted the tall tanned man, whose name was Norman Calder. City Councilman Norman Calder didn't need a button with his name and cause on it—he trusted his poise and oratory before the cameras, as well as his "Q" recognition factor for his many public appearances; and he wasn't about to be sucked into anything demeaning by a neighborhood housewife with no sense of scale and priorities.

Lydia Perez stuck out her chin toward him and waggled her finger. "What about the people who clean your houses and look after your kids?" she yelled, as camera noses appeared first over Calder's shoulder, then hers. "We have to commute from downtown every day, and most of us don't have cars."

Norman kept his voice lower, but enunciated better. "Buses run every ten minutes, honey. And nobody is telling you where to work or what to do. We're all in this together; we have to think about the future of this great city."

A woman carrying a Starbucks bag in which were two Styrofoam cups of what she considered to be some of the world's finest coffee (a raggedy man had just begged from her a handout, and she offered him instead a drink of fine coffee) raised her free hand and said, "Right on!"

Calder smiled over at her and mouthed, "Thank you, Hollis."

"Cut the crap, honey!" Lydia Perez bellowed. "The future is now, and we ain't in this together until we get to get around this place just as good as you!"

"There's no reasoning with you people," Norman Calder said, comparatively quietly, looking directly into the lens over his opposite's shoulder. "There's always somebody opposing a positive change in policy."

"The only positive change I got, man, is what I need to ride this subway once they open it up to us with this stop here."

"Meanwhile"—Norman Calder sighed loudly enough to bring approving nods from the group on his side—"just ruin the environment, screw up the city, think only of yourselves."

"Oh, I think of you, too, every time I ride that stinkin' bus an hour and a half, man, to get to your neighborhood and do your shopping and clean your toilets—bet on it!"

Overall, despite this confrontation, L.A. did seem to be in a positive frame of mind. Subway lines were starting to reach out—at least on maps—red, green, blue. More water was siphoned off the Colorado (in hard bargaining with Las Vegas, which threatened to close its borders), and storm drains

were multiplying to handle torrents of muddy
runoff that seemed to be increasing from the sur-
rounding mountains. Angelinos were moving their
city ahead without fear; they had lived with slides
and shudders and threats for so long.

A few blocks away, in the prim and modest residential area of Crescent Heights, south of Olympic
Boulevard, a two-block section was barricaded off
for the operation of heavy equipment that had torn
up the street and continued chewing up the rock
and dirt below pavement level—not for a subway
stop, but for one of those storm-drain extensions
that so irked people while they were being built
and so gladdened them when sudden wild runoffs
no longer carried away their lawns and small pets.
Hung here and there from the barricades were
pleasant sheet-metal signs, white letters on a blue
background, proclaiming "Hollyhills Storm Drain
Extension".

As jackhammers hacked at pavement farther
along, and Case backhoes scooped out huge buck-
etfuls of rock and asphalt, a Komatsu crane lowered
an eight-foot metal plate over one section of the
excavation where the digging was complete.
Autocar diesel dump trucks idled in a row, to be
filled one by one from the wide maws of
International front-loaders which charged into piles

made by the backhoes and retreated with their tons of debris for the trucks. From exhaust pipes on all the various roaring machines came occasional belches of black fumes, and the air was filled with dark dust on which the morning sun sparkled.

In a white Craftsman-style bungalow overlooking this racketing dig, Kelly Roark lay in bed staring at the ceiling, from which wiggled a mobile of red and green fish—which had arrived through the mail a month before as a gift from her mother for Kelly's thirteenth birthday. She missed her mother sometimes, but was also aware that what she missed sometimes was not so much her mother as the "normal" family life she thought they had had before the divorce. She missed St. Louis, a little. Here, as there, most of her friends were now growing up shunted between divorced parents. Not so bad. Most of them lived with their mothers. Kelly liked living with her father. Except that he worked all the time.

At this exact moment, though, she missed the steadiness of their early life, which did not include the horrendous constant daytime din of the construction outside, and the time when her father did not work so much on improving L.A. In a brief lull, she heard the irate, gruff voice of their neighbor, Mr. Granelli, giving it to the construction crew. She rolled over and raised up on her elbow to look out the window. There he was, the fat tub, waving his arms as if directing a symphony, and two sweating hard hats were shrugging and not giving a damn, but listening nonetheless. She was wearing a "Dodgers" T-shirt, given to her by her sort-of-boyfriend Randall, who thought he was being supportive. She'd like to see Randall today, but not all that much. She felt she'd moved beyond St. Louis and its Randalls.

Disneyland. That was the promise for today. Who cared about Disneyland? Well, Dad was doing his best. She'd believe it when she saw it.

"Kel?" called her father from down the hall. "Breakfast."

The only reason she'd eat breakfast is so she didn't become anorexic, like a couple of her friends. A dump truck rumbled in, drowning out Mr. Granelli. But when the dump truck stopped, a faint rumbling continued for a few seconds. Could it be . . . an *earthquake*? Could it? She'd love it if it were. She'd not experienced one yet, and she wanted to feel sophisticated, able to accept as casually as everybody else did the occasional shakes of the earth. Even an aftershock would be okay, but she guessed you had to have an earthquake first.

Anyway, it probably wasn't anything, just another disappointment. "This city is like so lame," she said aloud.

Mike Roark, having been a single father for only a couple of years, was not entirely organized or confident about it. Out in their small backyard, he unhooked from the fig tree the leash of Max, the dachshund, wiped his hands on his clean St. Louis Cardinals T-shirt, noticed the stains, said "Damn!" and led Max into the kitchen. He called to Kelly that breakfast would be ready in half a mo.

At forty (no small tremor he had felt three months ago when he crossed that threshold, suddenly recognizing anew that he was aging, had a daughter, was discombobulated by being single), he was a still-firm five-eleven, weighed only five pounds more than he had when he wrestled in college, had all his hair—and teeth, he would remark ironically. Just not all his wits, he sometimes thought. He felt frazzled and wasn't sure why.

His job as director of the Office of Emergency Management was demanding, but he felt in control there. It was outside the office, little things that kept him off-balance. Kelly was unpredictable, even mercurial, from his point of view. He couldn't anticipate her likes and dislikes from one month to the next.

Max waited patiently, perched on his short front legs. Mike kept one eye on the small countertop TV, which was broadcasting a live report from the site of the protest over the proposed subway stop near the Beverly Center—he thought both sides were full of it, but it was interesting to see what roused people's passions. And his ears were full of the pounding, rattling, screeching, chugging construction work outside his own house. He put a skillet on the stove and turned on the burner. Next to the stove he flipped open a city guide to where he had circled Disneyland on the map. He took a can opener from the top drawer and opened a Dog Chow. The can squirted from his hands and plopped top down on the floor in front of Max. Max looked puzzled.

"Don't worry about it," Mike said, scooping the chow into Max's bowl.

Usually, on a Saturday morning, Mike would ask Kelly what she'd like for breakfast, and usually she said, "I don't know." Today, Monday, the first day of his week's vacation, he decided to risk fried eggs, without asking. It was riskier than he thought. When he cracked the first one into the now-over-heated pan it bubbled instantly into brown lace. Start over.

He didn't recognize the distinct rumble at first. It wasn't the construction that made the floor shiver.

"Stand in the doorway!" he hollered to Kelly. As a responsible father, he had made ready for L.A. He yanked open a cabinet door and quickly assessed the stash: flashlight, batteries, bottled water, canned food, Ibuprofen.

It was quickly over. There had been no pause in the noisy work outside.

Kelly straggled in. "That was a quake, right?"

"Yeah. Pretty good one, depending where. Not bad here, though. You don't have to worry."

"My first quake, and I couldn't even hear it, all that crappy noise outside."

"Be glad it wasn't bigger."

"Since the kitchen's still standing," she said, "I'm ready to eat."

"It'll be a minute."

"Already smells like burnt."

"Don't worry about it."

Actually, Mike thought there was a good chance that it was a substantial quake, epicentered a hundred miles away or something, and he half expected the phone to ring.

2
MAGMA

Actually, this magma plume was not just as Professor Heim had imagined and drawn in the classroom. This actual plume was larger, less regular, like an enormous amoeba, and followed and forced open cracks and paths and channels in a less predictable pattern on its massive voyage to the crust. It was alive, as the earth was alive. Its movement was both a product and a cause of the minute shifts in the plates that overlapped and rubbed and ground upon each other in their formation atop the crust of the earth. The magma— molten rock, propelled by gases under horrific pressures, roiled upward, finding slivers of room, forcing open fissures. The voyage of thousands of miles took years. Sometimes the magma was stopped, bound by impenetrable rock. But there was always movement, immeasurable, inexorable, in the rock of the crust, as massive tectonic plates heaved and slid in so enormous and ponderous a way as to be incomprehensible and unfelt by people on the surface. And always the magma sought the surface.

From this mysterious netherworld, scant intelligence reached the human beings on the surface. Only patterns could be detected—the Hawaiian Island chain, the mid-Pacific, the eastern rim, the faults that riddled California just below the sod. Where the plates skidded in tiny jots of distance over eons, hot spots below these thicknesses of crust remained, roaring to the surface through what were, in geophysical terms, tiny fissures between the plates. Earthquakes and volcanoes were not unrelated. The awesome forces that moved and shaped the earth were caused by heat and were the way heat was let loose, allowing the center of the earth to sweat and cool. The plates moved, the earth quaked, magma sought the soft spots. The earth breathed, the skin moved, the superheated plasma bubbled up.

But just where the magma plumes were, when they were tens of thousands of miles deep, and where they were headed, was not known above. How each plume selected its route was not known. Just where and when the magma would explode through the surface was not known until virtually as it happened—in geological terms, just when it happened. Nor could it be known whether the emersion would take the shape of a massive explosion that shot gas and steam and rocks thousands of feet into the sky, or whether the lava would roll out calm as molasses, or whether superheated groundwater, boiled by the rising magma, would blast out of the magma mouth along with carbon dioxide and nitrogen and other gases that would roll away in a noxious cloud under which no mammal or bug could breathe.

Mankind didn't know what, if anything, it did to affect the paths or nature of faults and flues. Underground atomic testing? Mining? The blasting of deep tunnels under cities for tubes to carry people or water or wires? What force from down deep might finally seek these conduits, the easy way out at the end of the long journey for the forces that shaped the earth?

Angelinos felt dozens of earthquakes a year, from a score of faults that ran north-south or east-west. The Pacific Plate was sliding under the thicker, lighter continental plate at the west coast—California. Anywhere the crust buckled and shifted, where the friction yielded such heat and vapors, underneath that was an opportunity for magma to escape. Los Angeles was busy blasting tubes under the ground above and along the most volatile piece of crust in North America.

Dr. Jaye Calder burst through the swinging doors to the emergency room and headed straight for the latest arrival. St. Vincent's was humming with the results of mean spirits on city streets. The emergency room was full, busy, and bloody. In a handful of years, maybe by the time she was forty, Jaye would not have the stomach for it anymore. But now she was intent on helping the wounded, those in the most distress, and, so long as she was in charge, this zoo was going to be run efficiently and lives would be saved. Even if it meant she would be tired all the time and weariness would age her pretty face and cause veins to surface in her long legs.

On the table lay the latest of the wounded, an unconscious middle-aged man whose shirt was soaked with blood. Paramedics and nurses scrambled around the table hooking up IVs and heart monitor, announcing readings, cutting away his clothes.

"Drive-by shooting on Hoover," a paramedic announced.

"Was County full?" Jaye asked. A victim from that location wouldn't usually be brought here.

"County *and* Kaiser. They had a busy weekend down there."

Jaye sighed and began examining the new patient. "How many exit wounds?"

"Two," the nurse said, tracing with her index finger. "Here and here."

"We've got some respiration, at least, a weak pulse." Jaye cast a quick eye over the procedures—the crew was efficient. The job was impossible these days. Everybody out there had guns. Some nights from in here it seemed like everybody out there was getting shot.

Suddenly one of the machines seemed to hop an inch. Then another slid a few inches. Only then did Jaye feel the tremor under her feet.

"Quake!" a nurse called.

Two nurses ducked under the operating table. The paramedics sprang toward the protective door-frames. Jaye stepped to the table and bent over it, shielding the injured man, her eyes never leaving the heart monitor. Its trolley started to roll, and she grabbed across for its handle, at the same time using her other hand to hold in the plug. Nothing totally unfamiliar so far, just always scary because you never knew whether this one, or the next, or the next, would be the "big one," the promised epic that would open up a vast chasm in the crust and swallow up L.A.

The shaking stopped. It was not a big one. The crew returned to its jobs briskly, but still with each person just the slightest bit tentative as usual, never sure whether five minutes from now a bigger shock would rattle them.

In the Roark kitchen, the phone did ring, and a voice from Mike's office informed him that it might have been a 6.2, and strange reports were coming in.

He grabbed a blue windbreaker, across the back of which yellow letters spelled out: "L.A. Emergency." Over the left breast pocket was a seal on which was the message "Los Angeles City Office of Emergency Management." He pulled on the jacket and snapped off the TV.

"Hey!" Kelly reacted, reaching for the switch. "I was watching!"

"Grab a jacket, we're going downtown."

"*Hello*? This is *vacation*. Can't you just do it over the phone? Like tell people what to do? Nothing really happened."

"This is my first quake too, honey. I gotta be there, make sure everything goes right."

"Even if nothing happened?" Kelly leaned back in her chair and folded her arms.

"We don't know if anything happened or not. I'm going just to make sure. Come on, we'll be back in an hour. Still hit Disneyland by noon."

"Who wants Disneyland? I told you, the deal is

OJ's house and the Beverly Center, like you promised."

"We said Disneyland. Anyway, we'll discuss it in the car."

He opened the door and looked back. She hadn't moved.

"Come on."

"I'm gonna wait here. Mom said she might call me this morning anyway."

"Might."

"Hey."

"Sorry. Don't get cranky. Come on, Kel, gimme a break. I don't want to worry about you."

"Then don't go in."

"This is my job, Kel."

"Yeah, but it's always your job. Just go ahead. I'll be okay." She brightened a little. "I will."

He smiled at her, and she smiled back. "If there's an aftershock—"

"I *know*, Dad, the doorframe. Go do your mysterious job. Whatever we have time for later will be okay."

"You're a princess. Thanks."

In his red Dodge Dakota pickup headed downtown, Roark was quickly grateful to leave the construction noise behind. He slowly rolled his head around, trying to relax his neck. "Jeez," he said aloud, "some father. Not even any breakfast."

The city amused him sometimes, amazed him often. Amused him because of its idiosyncrasies, its maddening casualness and insouciance, its seriousness about its industry—Hollywood—its playful rejection of the facts of its situation: there shouldn't even be a city on this desert coastal plain atop a thousand geological faults; where the sea fog, so persistent and thick the Spaniards used to call this area the "Bay of Smokes," now combined with man's effluents to make smog so bad that on some days it was hard and even unhealthy just to breathe; where, without importation of water over vast distances, there would be neither oranges nor faucets. Amazed him for its determined personality and belief in itself, its ability to create reality out of fantasy—not even palm trees were natural here—how many beautiful and talented people lived here, and how much money there was around this beautiful, warm, seductive place.

And there was the amazing paradox that the same nature that made this area so appealing was the nature that could cause, in an instant, the devastation that made this area famous for its fragility.

All in all, L.A. was defying the odds and having a wonderful time. What he liked most about being here were the challenges that this job promised. L.A. was, geologically speaking, an unstable place. In addition to the normal emergencies that hit large metropolises—storms, power outages, street flooding, and so on—

earthquakes were common, mud slides from the mountains, fires in the mountain and valley scrub and woodlands. Not that he had a morbid interest in such disasters, just that when they happened, he liked to be on the scene, calling the shots, fixing problems, organizing forces, helping people—an intimate witness to dramas of life and death.

The ultimate, of course, was to save lives. He had once saved a life, directly. Not a person, but at least a life. When he was ten, a farm kid, he had plunged into the roiling floodwaters of the Missouri, which sloshed and swirled around him shoulder high, to lead a bawling Jersey heifer out to higher ground. He had been praised and chastised: praised because it had been a brave act, chastised because it had been foolhardy, and he could have just as easily drowned himself.

The farmer whose heifer it was said, "Thanks, you done a brave thing." Mike's father had said, "It was a damn fool thing to do. My boy does some dumb things." His mother had held his soaked, shaking body, and said, "Promise me you'll never do anything like that again."

But Mike just sat on the levee the next day and watched the big river and thought that what he had done was neither heroic nor stupid; it was natural. It was the most natural thing in the world for him to spring to help. He was drawn as naturally to that as a moth to light—or flame.

When he was studying for his master's in Urban Control at Butler, he lived in the little town of Biscuit Bend and was a volunteer fireman. He had, in fact, met his wife in the line of work—not saved her life in this case, but at least led her out of the smoking trailer which was the hair salon where she did perms, and helped her get her breath back. In gratitude and admiration she had gone out with him, and then she married him. But gradually over time, as they had Kelly and Kelly grew, while Mike had pursued action and salvation in urbia, she had longed again for small towns and simplicity and safety. In time that came to mean more than the fact that Mike had once led her out of a smoking salon; moreover, he wasn't around enough to be helpful to Kelly, or to her, and she happened to meet the owner of a combine dealership back home in Indiana and took off with him.

It was that last event that would lead to the legal determination that Kelly was better off with the upright father, Mike. The grudge Mike held was not composed so much of angers as disappointments. She was not a bad woman, not cheap or irresponsible; she was just lonely and impatient. She hadn't been willing to wait for Mike to get his bellyful of disasters and retreat to a cabin in the country. Mike had told her he would, one day, have enough of it, get tired. But even as he had promised it over and over again, he had never been sure, deep down.

As he moved through traffic toward his office, he wondered whether he was lonely for female companionship or not. He wondered whether he could truly share his life. He didn't want to succumb to the temptation just to get somebody to help him with Kelly. But Kelly did need a woman's touch. Maybe he did, too.

He wouldn't have even thought these thoughts if this morning's incident and summons to the office had been anything more than a minor dust-up, hardly more than routine. He felt a little guilty for having so eagerly sprung into action when he had promised Kelly the day.

While the shock he had felt at his house this morning might turn out to be nothing, it provided a good dry run for practice; sooner or later he would have to help the city recover from some major blow delivered by nature.

3

HEAT UNDER THE CITY

In the basement of the new Metropolitan Transit Authority building—seven stories of blue concrete with white letters and white-framed windows, a frieze showing the shapes of a classic old automobile, a steam locomotive, a trimotor airplane, and crossed pickaxes over the wide front doors—the staff manning the brain center was quietly intense. Dominating the main wall was a huge electronic grid map of all transit routes in the city. Closed-circuit monitors flashed scenes of dark subway tracks. Radios crackled with messages back and forth from drivers and supervisors.

Twenty engineers were focused on the three

subway routes. Evidence of what caused their intensity was minor—coffee stains on their shirts and slacks, a couple of chairs rolled into each other in the corner, a pile of manuals tipped over and sprawled. The engineers leaned forward on their elbows, some swiveling nervously in their chairs.

Behind them paced Stan Olber, a bulky, sober man who, at fifty, was the oldest in the room. He had personally brought two engineers into this operation to serve under him. It was a smooth operation. Olber, nearly bald, a sturdy six-one, with wire-rimmed glasses perched on the end of his nose, was a firm commander.

"We got any power failures?" he barked as he strode behind the chairs.

"Blue Line running," answered one engineer.

"Green Line good."

"Ditto Red, main and auxiliary."

Olber rubbed his chin. "Radio contact with the trains?"

"Radio up and running on Blue."

"Green up and running."

"Red operational."

Olber nodded and continued pacing. Just as he thought, this was not going to be much of a problem. But he liked the way the men were right on top of things. "Okay, then let's get down to business." He allowed himself a slight smile. "Epicenter and magnitude. Who's in for a buck?"

Engineers relaxed in their seats, looked around, several calling out their guesses at once:

"Norwalk, 4.6." "Whittier Narrows, 3.9." "Inglewood, 3.4." "Sylmar, 5.0." "Vegas, 6.8."

The last pick drew hoots and smirks, and the engineer who volunteered his guess that it had been a big one at Vegas taunted with his smile and waved a dollar bill.

Olber chuckled. "Harry, you're an optimist. Take more than what we felt this morning to account for a 6.8 in Vegas. Okay, everybody, we'll be all right. Radios open for a while, though, let 'em run. Let's make sure we got no cracks in the cradle."

Olber walked back and forth, watching the blinking lights and the screens. For some reason, he felt edgy as a ferret.

Professor Alan Heim pumped his bicycle down Fourth Street past Sweetzer, on his way to the Farmers Market on the corner of Third and Fairfax. He didn't like the Farmers Market because he didn't like crowds, and he didn't like shopping, not for any reason. What drew him to the Farmers Market was Dr. Rachel Wise. What drew him to Rachel Wise was not just the usual things—looks, brains, sensitivity—but the added alluring factors of her elusiveness and her absolute refusal to go out with him.

He'd spent seven years, ever since his divorce, not having anything to do with women. Lately he'd decided it was time to end his bachelor brooding and look for some companionship.

He had met Rachel Wise at a campsite not far from Great Bear, just stumbled across her tent, which it turned out was not far from his tent. She had black, pixieish hair, muscular legs, and a captivating, fleeting smile. She was packing up to leave, and they chatted just long enough for him to find out that she was a seismologist, and he decided just to take a shot.

She'd said: "I don't think so. I . . . I . . . I'm very busy with my work, and, uh, well . . . that's about it."

Maybe she's had some bad experiences, he'd thought.

But then she'd said, "It's awfully nice of you to ask."

"I'll call you," he said.

"Okay," she said.

He'd called and called, she was always "busy." Except this time she'd said, "I'm going by the Farmers Market tomorrow, early."

The road shook, and Professor Heim lost control and shot off the street into a royal palm. He went over the handlebars into the tree, and when he got his bearings he was sitting under the tree with a broken nose.

He laughed, because pain was no problem for

him. "She may be cursed"—he chuckled—"but she won't get away from me."

"Come on, Rache," Ken Woods, the associate PR director, pleaded. "How tough can it be?"

"Tough enough," muttered Dr. Rachel Wise in a trembling voice, peeking from behind an offstage door not far from her lab. Waifish in her green lab smock and close-cropped dark hair, she was, at thirty-three, painfully uncomfortable with almost anything outside of her machines and gauges and scopes—especially anything to do with the press.

Woods tried to press a memo into her hand. "Come on."

"I can't."

"It's just a couple of sentences. Maybe a question or two."

"Then you do it."

"When the ground moves, people want to hear from a seismologist, not a pencil pusher."

It was like her first date, when her roommate had pressed her into meeting this guy, and she had already resolved that dating would be altogether too difficult and time-consuming and scary, and that she could easily do without it, but she had for some reason agreed and now was reneging and refusing to come out of her room.

She had finally gone on that date, and it had been agony.

"My contract doesn't force me to do the press."

"Oh, cut it out, Rache. Jesus. I'm beggin' you."

"If I go out there, I'll throw up."

"Well, that might not have quite the calming effect we'd hoped."

"Well, that's what. . . thank God!"

Dr. Amy Barnes, her lab boss, was hurrying down the hall, smock flying out behind her, one sneaker untied.

"Morning, Doctor," Woods said, nodding. Glancing back to Rachel, he said, "You're off the hook, Star."

"Hey, Rache," Amy said. "Got here as fast as I could."

Woods handed her the memo, nodded at them both, blew kisses, and walked toward the auditorium.

Amy studied the memo; Rachel peered over her shoulder. The two could have been twins, the major visible difference being that Rachel was less disheveled. But the major difference really was that Amy didn't have any nerves. The press didn't bother her at all—she hardly thought of them as people. It was the press of time that caused her distraction.

"Six point two," she read, "Mojave Desert, eighty miles northeast of the Civic Center. That's it?"

"That's it," Rachel said, feeling sheepish.

"Got it. See you in a minute."

"Uh, Amy?" Rachel said quietly. "I got some stuff I want to show you later, okay?"

"Okay." Amy strode off toward the auditorium, where a handful of the usual beat reporters awaited what they always hoped would be more dramatic than it almost ever turned out to be.

Rachel watched her go, envious of Amy's calm, detached professionalism. She'd love to relax like that, just be at ease among people. Or be even better at her job, so she'd feel more confident. She was not exactly sure, for example, about the squiggles on her graphs this morning. The 6.2 was there, clear enough. But there were some strange marks, tiny flutters, and there were some vague reports of odd temperature readings. Nothing really. Yet she felt she was missing something, for some reason. If she were better at her job, she wouldn't miss anything, or if there weren't anything to miss, she wouldn't feel as if she were missing it.

Ah, well, at least she hadn't had to face the press—that would be worse than any quake.

A crowd of neighborhood people gathered outside the First A.M.E. Church, where, at the dead end of Whitworth at Curson, a BMW 740 had rear-ended a Honda Accord driven by DeNiece Stock, a trim woman in a business suit who happened to be a member of the church and was irately invoking the name of a vengeful God by the time the police cruiser slowly rolled to a stop and two officers got out and put on their hats.

The two officers, both under thirty, were about the same age as Ms. Stock, but, unlike her, they were white. Bud McVie and Terry Jasper had been on this beat just two months.

They approached her through the murmuring crowd with casual wariness, and McVie addressed the woman.

"Morning, ma'am. Can you tell me what's going on here?"

"Yeah I can. Some white boys slammed into my car."

"That would be this second vehicle here, the BMW."

The BMW, empty, was now wedged in by two other cars that had blocked it from the rear.

"You got that right. That's it. Radio said we were havin' a quake, so I hit my brakes, and I tell you, brakes on this Honda work a damn sight better than on that BMW. And these guys hit me from behind. I'm cool. I get out to get their insurance shit, and they make it a racial thing! They come right out and say I'm hassling them because they're stuck in a black neighborhood. Can you imagine?"

"Hmm," McVie said.

"Guy coming," Jasper said, nudging him.

Pastor Theosophus Lake emerged through the dark double doors of the whitewashed church and came deliberately down the steps. Peeking out the doors behind him were three sets of eyes above white cheeks.

"That's them!" DeNiece said, pointing. "They hit me and hid in there."

The crowd grumbled. Pastor Lake spread his arms. "People, people, it's all right."

A boy in his late teens stepped up behind DeNiece, waving a fist. "Get them punks outta there!"

"You tell 'em, Kevin. Kevin here's my brother, Officers. He was in the car with me."

"People, people," Pastor Lake intoned, as the three pairs of wide eyes disappeared, and the doors closed behind him.

Officer Jasper held up a hand in front of Kevin, who shook his head.

"That's our church, man!"

"Yeah. . . yeah. . . yeah!" growled the crowd.

"How many times you been in it, Kevin?" came a voice from the crowd, followed by laughter.

"Yeah, well, fuck you, too, man."

Pastor Lake stepped between them and announced in his soft, deep voice, addressing the officers: "The boys won't come out without an escort."

"I'll get 'em out!" hollered Kevin.

"Knock it off," Officer McVie said, as the crowd surged around them.

A bottle smashed on the street behind them, and the officers jumped.

"Let's get some backup," Officer McVie stage-whispered to Officer Jasper.

"Roger that."

They headed for their cruiser.

Back inside the church, Pastor Lake said to the boys, all three juniors at Azuza State, "You have refuge here, of course. Sanity will be restored outside, after which you will have your penance for the damage you caused. There is no charge for your cowardice. You can make yourselves useful, however."

He led them forward toward the altar. Glass glittered below the podium. "Fortunately, the tremor we had this morning caused only the toppling of a candelabrum and the resultant mess of altar candles. Clean it up."

By ten-thirty, Roark had reached the glass door of his office, on which were painted the words: "Michael Roark—OEM Director". He opened the door and stopped short.

Seated behind his desk, with his feet propped up on it, was Emmit Reese.

"My, my, aren't we comfortable."

Reese instantly removed his feet from the desk top and sat forward and laced his fingers. "It is so *you* to blow a vacation day for a wimpy little tremor."

"My first."

"Another couple months you'll be used to them."

"I won't be used to you taking over my office."

"Sorry, just waiting. What happened with Disneyland?"

Roark grabbed a clipboard. Emmit Reese was only twenty-five, very bright, wiry, energetic. A good assistant. Olber had recommended him when Roark suggested the office looked a little lily white. Only problem was, he was superambitious. Maybe that wasn't a problem either. They just had to get used to each other. "If a dam broke somewhere and the mayor called, I didn't want you telling her, 'Mike's at Disneyland.'"

"The mayor's in Gstaad. We don't pull her off the slopes for a 6.2. Anyway"—Roark started out, and Reese sprang up to follow—"I'd cover for you."

"Uh-huh."

Reese chuckled at the cynicism, trying to keep pace as Roark whizzed along the corridor.

A staffer grabbed Reese's sleeve and hooked a thumb in the direction Roark passed. "I thought he had the week off."

"Yeah. What can I tell you? The man likes to hover."

"Like he doesn't trust us to handle things."

"Well, it's his head." Reese charged away, with a quick wave.

Roark bumped into a technician coming out of an office. "We lose any gas mains?"

"Gas, power, phones all up," the man answered briskly, falling into step beside Roark. "We've got a little problem with a water main in Pacoima."

"What's a little problem?"

"Seepage, is all. Not big, not deep. Traffic can move. They said they had it covered."

"Don't forget about it. Stay on it. Keep it little."

"You bet."

The man peeled off into another office, poking his head back out as Reese passed. Reese gave him the thumbs-up while the man waggled his hand as if it had been singed.

At the southeast corner of MacArthur Park, near the corner of Seventh and Alvarado, Willy-Willy guffawed and poked Pooch in the ribs. The two homeless men were sitting on the ground watching three city people argue by a manhole out in the street. "City people" were what they called anybody who worked for the city. In this case a traffic cop—a chubby black woman—was barking at two Department of Public Works guys wearing blue jumpsuits and yellow hard hats.

"I don't care what your super says," the cop

snarled, waggling her finger at the DPW van occupying a traffic lane behind a "V" of orange pylons. "Nobody ran a work order by me, and my job is to keep any unauthorized vehicle from blocking traffic, and this vehicle is blocking traffic!"

"What're you gonna do?" the man with "Del" stitched on his pocket sneered. "Ticket us with a city vehicle?"

"How 'bout maybe I tow your ass, honey? I'll have it hauled out of here, tools and all, legal as Christmas, and you can walk downtown and argue it out there. How 'bout that?"

She took her radio out of her rear pocket. Willy-Willy and Pooch quietly laughed and laughed, holding their ribs.

"She'll do her, too, she will," Pooch said.

"Bet to that, mister!" They elbowed each other. It wasn't often they had such entertainment to pass the time. In fact, while there had been a couple of stabbings in the park, punches thrown here and there, stuff stolen right and left, a little sex to watch once in a while, there hadn't been such righteous official haggling before their eyes since they had more or less taken up residence here three months ago. The quake this morning had just rocked them back to sleep, and they were glad the noise over here woke them up so they didn't miss it.

"Looky that!" Pooch suddenly pointed. "Yellow smoke!"

A yellow-orange gas was belching out of the manhole in thick puffs, and in the middle of it a hand reached up, and a voice was gasping something.

The DPW men spun from the traffic cop, leaped to the hole, and grasped the hand. "What the . . . Carlos! What the hell?" They yanked him up, and he collapsed to the pavement, twitching, barely breathing, while the workers gaped for a moment.

"Get an ambulance!" Del screamed at the cop, who was already running to her car.

They carefully turned Carlos over. His face was scorched black. Clothes were melted to his body. "Jesus Christ!" Chuck whispered.

"Carlos!" Del said, leaning his face close to the injured man's, disregarding the ugliness and stink. "What the hell happened down there? Can you talk? Can you hear me?"

Carlos tried to speak, blood gurgled up instead. Del cradled his head.

"Oh man oh man oh man . . ."

"You're gonna be awright, buddy," Chuck said, fidgeting with his hands, not knowing what to do with them. "It'll just be a minute. Just hold on, buddy."

Already there were sirens—police, the men could tell. Ambulance would be right behind them.

"What about the other guys?" Del asked. "Carlos, the other guys. Can you hear me? Oh Jesus oh shit."

Carlos began to move his mouth. Del leaned his ear down.

"They're gone," Carlos rasped. "They're gone. So hot . . . burned . . . I couldn't . . . I couldn't . . ."

His head lolled to one side.

4
CASUALTIES

It was nearly midday, and the tropical sun beat down on seven black body bags lying in a row on the black asphalt near the manhole at the corner of MacArthur Park. Two fire trucks, several Public Works vehicles, two ambulances, and a scattering of police squad cars surrounded the scene. The whole area was cordoned off with crime-scene tape and traffic cones. No traffic approached the intersection. When hell had almost literally broken loose, Willy-Willy and Pooch quietly fled the scene: experience told them that when bodies appear, it was time to split.

Roark arrived in his big white Chevy Suburban "L.A. City OEM" van and paused a moment behind the wheel, surveying the grim scene, before getting out. "Jesus H. Christ," he mumbled, exhaling a long sigh.

He tucked a rolled-up map under his arm, stepped out, and tapped the shoulder of a hard hat. "Where's Lapher?"

The man gestured toward the other side of the manhole, where a heavyset man with thick glasses, wearing a blue windbreaker and a yellow "DPW" helmet, was standing.

Roark cast a long look at the row of body bags as he walked over. "Hello, Roger."

"What're you doing here?" He spat off to the side.

"The call said you lost seven men. What ha—"

"Freak accident on a storm-drain job. That's all. It's under control now." Lapher didn't meet Roark's eyes.

"That's it?"

"Right."

"That what you're putting in your report? 'Freak accident'?"

Lapher folded his arms and spat again. "They hit a steam pocket and got scalded. No explosion, no fire. Closed off. Done. No continuing threat. No threat!" Now he looked at Roark. "We'll copy you on the report."

"Thanks."

Lapher was so damned insecure. Threatened by everything and everybody. Roark would be glad when he retired—he was already in his sixties, and covering his ass every which way.

Roark walked over to the body bags. A cop was

kneeling beside the closest one, entering something on a notepad. The cop looked up.

"Open it," Roark said softly.

The cop pulled the zipper down. The man's face was red and black. His clothes were in rags. His rubber boots were singed brown and melted around his feet, covering them like chocolate on an Eskimo Pie.

Roark nodded, and the cop zipped the bag back up. Roark ambled back to Lapher, who was staring off into the park. "Steam did that?"

Lapher shrugged. "You ever see what live steam can do?"

"Where's the survivor?"

"Saint Vincent's. Critical, last time I checked. Third-degree burns all over. Probably blind. Poor bastard."

"Yeah." Roark nodded.

"But I'd like to notify the families before they hear about all this on *Geraldo*, so if you wouldn't mind . . ." Lapher raised his eyebrows questioningly.

"What?"

"Your office draws cameras like shit draws flies. I just wish you'd get your van the hell out of here."

"I like to see these things for myself, Roger."

"The other guy used to wait for a call."

"I'm not the other guy."

"Roark, we'll copy you."

Another vehicle pulled up near them, this one a

blue Bronco marked "Metro Transit Authority," and Stan Olber got out and headed directly for them.

Roark spoke first. "Stan, something I want you to see."

"Hey," Lapher groaned, "it's under control!"

Roark held up a calming hand and motioned for Olber to squat down with him. He unrolled the map, an underground grid of this section of the city. With his index finger he traced one of the thickened, meandering lines. "This is where our problem is."

"Was!" Lapher snapped down at them.

Roark fluttered his hand at him without looking up. He traced another line, one roughly parallel and quite close to the first. "This is your Red Line tunnel."

"Okay," Olber acknowledged, rubbing his chin. "So?"

"I'd like you to shut this section down."

"What?"

"Just a precaution. Until we know what's going on."

While Lapher moaned and stamped around, Olber sat up straight and was silent for a moment. Roark waited. He knew that Olber was too savvy to explode. He was reasonable, if conservative, like other bureaucrats protecting their turf.

Then Olber said, "Why should we look bad just because DPW blew up some pipes?"

"Nothing blew down there, Olber," Lapher whined. "They hit a steam pocket. You guys should be careful how you throw words around."

Olber looked up, his hands on his knees. "Steam? Steam can't get to my trains." He looked at Roark. "The tunnel walls are five feet of concrete. No way steam gets through that to my tubes."

"Maybe not before." Roark's beeper went off. He snatched it off his belt. His home number, Kelly. He sighed.

"Can we wrap this up?" Lapher whined.

"Maybe the tremor knocked something loose."

"We have these all the time," Olber said.

"Yeah. Could be cumulative. Could be something else. I heard about yellow smoke, in bursts. I don't know. Let's find out before we—"

"It's over!" Lapher snapped. Roark shot him a fierce look, and he winced. "Would you stop treating this like an ongoing emergency, please?" When Olber glared, too, he held up his palms, turned away, and got into his car. "I gotta get to the hospital before you guys create a docudrama out here!"

Olber ignored him and rubbed his chin. "Thirty thousand people think they're taking trains home tonight. What am I supposed to do about them?"

"How about extra buses?"

Olber looked pained. "It's his mess." He waggled a thumb at Lapher, who was accelerating away with a screech. "Let him take the shit for it."

"It's not the question," Roark said, "who takes the shit. It's who can protect the public. We got seven dead. You got thirty thousand riders."

Olber sighed and slowly exhaled through pursed lips.

A van screeched to a stop, and they whipped their heads around. Out of the door that announced "Continental Cablevision" a man with wildly windblown hair landed, wearing a tan sport jacket and red tie. "Roark!" he called, trotting over.

Roark closed his eyes.

"Which one of you geniuses melted my lines this morning?" the man growled, panting.

"Not now, Buddy," Roark said softly.

"Whaddya mean, not now? Now! We lost cable to seventy thousand homes. Fried! What the hell's that?" He pointed to the body bags, now being loaded into the coroner's trucks.

"We got a delicate problem, Buddy." Roark stood up, took the man's elbow, and steered him away toward his cable van.

"I gotta know who's gonna pay for my fried lines," the man persisted.

"Come by my office, okay? About an hour."

"Christ."

"An hour." Roark helped him in, shut the door, and walked away toward his own van, where Olber was waiting, nervously tapping Roark's rolled map into the palm of his hand.

By noon, Roger Lapher was peering intently

through the small window in the door to the emergency room at St. Vincent's.

The DPW worker Carlos was suspended in a sling over a stainless-steel tub half-full of antibiotic solution. He was mostly covered with medicated gauze, and rolls of gauze were piled up on a table. Once in a while he emitted a small moan.

Jaye daubed at an exposed piece of raw skin. "Blood pressure?"

"One-seventy over 105," the nurse responded.

"Increase the Procardia drip. Start the lactated Ringers." She glanced at the window. "Steam doesn't char tissue like this."

"Not hot enough?" offered the young intern who assisted.

"Not hot enough. Something else." She fingered an area above the man's ankles, where there was a yellow tinge. She sniffed it through her mask.

Lapher's eyes followed her. Sweat formed on her brow, sweat formed on his.

On the trawler *Susan L* five miles off Santa Monica, crewman Dave Raney spat into the bow wave and gazed eastward at the shore. "I been thinking," he said to the captain, his father, Bill.

"That's a change," Bill said.

"No, really. L.A. ain't what it used to be."

"Nothing is."

"But really."

"Who gives a shit?"

"Well"—Dave stroked his beard—"people raising kids, like that."

"Who's raising kids?"

"People do. The air sucks."

"What else is new?"

"But look. Look how it is this morning."

"Same old fucking haze and smog."

"It ain't. It's different. Got waves in it, like shimmering."

Captain Raney turned away, leaned back against the gunwale, and stared back out to sea, where they had had another bum night. He had, in fact, noticed the air over L.A., that it was different this morning, weird, overheated, vibrating shit. But he didn't want to think about it, couldn't deal with it. He'd already breathed it for sixty-eight years, whatever it was. His chest hurt. He ached for sleep. L.A. was either going to quake off and sink into the sea, or get covered with mountain mud, or blow up from some frigging technology, or croak from cars and bad air. Didn't matter. There were no more sardines in the sea, and damn few pilchards. That's what was going to kill him, not the damn air over L.A. His son was more curious because he had longer to live.

"Don't you see it, Dad? Right there in the middle, like shimmering. What you think it is?"

"Who gives a shit." He stalked off to climb the ladder to the bridge.

Captain Likakis's mouth looked like he was blowing smoke rings, and his eyes widened and narrowed.

"What the hell was that?" the flight attendant said, steadying herself against the back of his seat.

"Just thought I'd give you a bit of a wild ride on the way in," he said, leering back at her, "like I've always wanted to."

"Well, the turbulence seemed to surprise you, too."

"Nothing over L.A. surprises me anymore. Although I will admit—"

"Let's just set this bastard down," muttered the flight engineer from his console. "I never felt a seven-four-seven bounce like that."

"Okay, okay, you guys. Maybe we got the city jitters for the flyover. Whatever it was is behind us, just Pacific now. Set up for final."

"What's that, Mommy?" The little blond boy tugged on his mother's hand with one hand and pointed with the other.

"That's a mastodon, like an elephant," she said. "Just a model of what they looked like. Thousands and thousands of years ago they lived around here. They don't exist anymore."

"The LaBerry Tarbels stink."

"La Brea Tar Pits, dear. Way back those thousands of years ago, oil came up through cracks from deep in the earth and made pools here. Those ancient animals like mastodons used to come here to drink water, and a lot of them got caught in the tar. They fell in there and just got sucked down into the tar. Years and years ago, before any of us were born."

"Even you?"

"Even Grandpa."

"Dogs and cats?"

"Well, animals even older than them. Strange tigers and birds and—"

"Why's that bubble?"

"I don't see any bubble."

"There was, there was, right in there. It went glug."

"Well, this doesn't bubble. It's awfully warm all of a sudden. Do you feel warm?"

"There was a bubble."

"It probably looked like a bubble."

The little boy had seen a bubble. A small one had formed briefly. He thought he saw another one, but didn't want to say anything.

Beneath the surface, the tar was starting to move,

air was expanding. Inside the tar it was awfully warm all of a sudden. A haze was forming over the surface, dancing with the heat.

Five LAPD black-and-white squad cars—in one of which no-nonsense Lieutenant Bert Fox had been chauffeured to the scene—formed a "U" at the end of the entry sidewalk, and ten officers formed short twin phalanxes for a safe passageway from the church to Officer McVie's car. About fifty locals were still gathered around—many had gotten tired of it and left—to protest the protection of the three college juniors who had been in the BMW that hit DeNiece's Honda. As McVie and Jasper escorted the boys down the walk, the crowd came alive.

"Let 'em loose! Give 'em the treatment! Punks! Bang 'em up! Stay home!"

"See what I mean?" said one of the boys. "They're like animals."

"Just keep your head down," McVie said.

Two more bottles whistled down from apartment windows and smashed on the street.

DeNiece's brother Kevin winced. "This ain't right, I mean, throwing shit."

"They rammed my Honda," DeNiece asserted.

"Yeah, but. . ."

A tow truck began to move away, hauling the

BMW. Two boys lunged at the car with baseball bats, smashing the windows and headlights.

"Oh man," Kevin groaned. "We just get it back double."

Lieutenant Fox, who had been watching the procedure with his arms folded and his lower lip thrust out, grabbed a nightstick from one of the patrolmen and charged at the boys, waving the club, and they took off. He handed the club back to the officer and sauntered up to McVie and Jasper. "You guys got a knack for turning a minor incident into a riot."

The officers didn't answer as they put their hands on the heads of the students as if they were suspects and maneuvered them into the squad car.

"Okay, everybody!" The lieutenant stalked into the crowd with the assuredness of the Marine captain he had once been. "Get outta here! You know me. Don't push it. No more trouble on this day."

The crowd quickly began to disperse.

"Well, ole Fox is right," Kevin said to DeNiece, as they walked away. "At least it didn't hurt our church none, all this junk."

"'Less they left a odor," DeNiece sniffed.

"Know what? There is a kind of funny smell."

"That's them," DeNiece said.

The open manhole at the corner of Seventh and Alvarado was still cordoned off, but all the emergency vehicles and personnel and bodies were gone. Roark sat on a nearby bench in MacArthur Park—the same one earlier occupied by Willy-Willy and Pooch until the unfolding events frightened them away—and stared at the scene. It was almost as if nothing had happened. The manhole looked as innocent as any other, but not long ago, for eight men it had been the gateway to hell.

Halfway down the block a single squad car was parked along the curb, its officers keeping a quiet watch on the area. It was something Roark had asked for. Right now, he didn't trust anything under these streets. God, those men had been treated to an ugly death. He hadn't seen the injured man—what was his name?

He checked his watch. Where the hell were they? He hadn't eaten. What was supposed to be his first vacation day had certainly turned sour. He snapped his fingers and grimaced as he sprang to his feet, suddenly remembering. He trotted across the intersection to a phone booth and dialed home.

Busy. He waited, dialed again. Busy again. Well, better she was talking to somebody. Maybe her mom. Roark felt a twinge of jealousy. You never know what an ex-mate is telling your kid, how your kid is responding.

Then he saw the van pull up, a city OEM just like his. While he was trotting over, he saw Emmit Reese and Gator Harris get out.

Gator made him smile—even today. While Reese

was wired, wiry, and ambitious, Gator, while efficient, was laid-back, tubby, bearded.

"Ready when you are, Chief." Gator waved.

"Let's do it."

Emmit was slowly shaking his head. "This is
such a bad idea."

"Get used to it."

"But, you know, we aren't—"

"We gotta know what's down there, Emmit."

"So that's what Public Works crews are for."

"Like you said on the phone. But I don't feel like
waiting three days for their report. Do you?"

Emmit sighed and headed for the back of his
van. "Price you pay for being good at stuff is you
have to do everything."

"You got it, bro," said Gator, chuckling.

Emmit threw open the back of the van. Inside
were fire-fighting suits and other coverall outfits,
various types of boots, masks, Scott Air Packs, rows
of tools neatly hung. On a bench at one side was a
bank of radio equipment. "Okay, y'all get dolled up
and do what you gotta do."

5

SEARCHING BELOW

Roark, then Gator, reached the bottom metal rung of the ladder that descended straight down the manhole and stepped off. Roark moved off first, with Gator close behind him carrying an infrared heat sensor that resembled a police radar detector with a small screen. Their black fire-fighting outfits quickly became nearly invisible, except for the bright yellow stripes. Their face masks glinted in the last of the sun above, and their faces behind the masks quickly dripped with sweat. They flashed their lights into the eerie dark tunnel. The dank walls had splotches of moss and the flicking movements of bugs. "Yo, guys," came Reese's voice from the van console into Roark's helmet receiver. "How'm I coming in?"

Roark spoke into a mike Velcroed to the front of his suit. "Five-by-five. Heat's unbelievable down here. You okay, Gator?"

"Yeah, Chief, long as we don't have to run. I'm right behind you. Man, it's toasty in here. Is it too late to switch jobs with Emmit?"

"Negatory on that," came Emmit's voice. "Take it easy, guys, don't be in a hurry. You know how heat saps you."

Roark knew that the comment was directed mainly at Gator, who didn't have wide experience. Emmit didn't want to embarrass him. "We'll stay cool, Em."

They edged down the tunnel, flashing their beams around. Twenty-five yards away the pipeline came into view: a concrete tube twenty-five feet across, massive as a submarine in the tunnel. Roark shined his light up along the ceiling of the tunnel near the pipeline. Water beads glistened. *Steam?* he wondered.

He tilted his head down toward his mike. "We're closing on the pipeline now, maybe fifteen yards. There's a big hatch, open. This is where the bodies were, outside this hatch."

"Easy, guys," came Reese's voice.

They looked around the hatch. Mike tested the round wheel with which the hatch could be sealed; it turned easily. He felt around the edge of the hatch; no breaks.

Gator looked around. "Man, they musta died in a hurry, they got no farther out than this."

"Let's have a look inside."

"Man. That's a big mother pipe."

"Hey, Mike?" Reese radioed. "A call just came through for you. I'll patch it through."

"Take a message."

"Uh, no dice. It's Sindelar, Boss."

Wayne Sindelar was chief of police. An experienced man, tough, firm on rules and discipline, just a good bit short on patience.

Roark drew a slow breath through clenched teeth. "Put him through."

After some clicking, Chief Sindelar's voice came through fainter than Reese's. "What the hell are you doing down there?" the chief rasped without preamble.

Roark and Gator stepped through the hatch into the huge pipeline, built for water thirty years before, extending in either direction beyond the reach of their lights. Rust and sediment had built up to maybe a foot thick.

"You'll have to speak up, Wayne," Roark said, panting from the slight exertion, wiping his visor with the back of his glove. "I can barely hear you."

"Public Works told me they were sending a crew in!" Sindelar shouted.

"I didn't think it could wait, Chief. Didn't think it should wait."

"Hey, Roark, you ain't in Kansas anymore. Know what I'm saying?"

"St. Louis."

"What?"

"I'm from St. Louis."

"What the hell's that got to do with it?"

A laugh, not stifled quite enough, came over the open mike from the van.

"Come again, Chief?" The incoming voice was breaking up.

"Hey, Roark, are you listening to me? You hear me?"

"A little better now."

"Remember your job description? You got a desk now, Roark. That's where you work. Not down in the damn sewer."

They were advancing cautiously, playing their lights around the massive pipe, probably under MacArthur Park by now. Far down the tunnel, Gator's light caught a flash of white.

"There!" Roark brought his beam over and the two lights converged. "There's the steam vent."

"What steam vent?" came Sindelar's crackling voice. "What're you doing? What the hell's going on. Sit still!"

They moved along toward the flash of white. The flash of white became a thin jet spewing up into the pipe.

"Lapher had it right," Roark said. "We've got steam coming through a crack in the bottom of the pipeline. Tremendous heat."

Condensation clouded their face masks quicker than they could wipe it away. Sweat poured down inside their suits. Roark felt a little light-headed.

"Gator?"

"I'm okay, I'm okay." He was nearly gasping, trying to stay under control.

They felt a rumble. A deep, long, shake, then it had a sound that grew.

"Aftershock?"

"Subway, Gator. We're right up against it."

It became a roar, then faded; the ground calmed. The men neared the vent. They both sucked for air, gulped.

"You copying me?" Sindelar asked, the transmission cracking. "I'm not just gonna sit . . ."

The voice was breaking up. Roark, moving ahead of Gator, using one hand in a vain attempt to keep his visor clear, put the other hand to the side of his helmet, pushing it closer to hear. Just a squeal now. He leaned to his mike. But the mike was a sagging piece of plastic—melting.

Roark couldn't see, couldn't hear, was awash in sweat so heavy he could feel his feet slosh in his boots. "Holy shit—"

They were fifteen feet away when the vent blew.

A gusher of yellow gas exploded from the crack in the floor, so hot and powerful it knocked Roark straight backward and down. In the instant he gaped into it he saw it swirl and spark, saw a rat hurled toward him, only to pop like a balloon in midair.

Gator was on him immediately, yanking him to his feet.

"Go!" Roark yelled.

They ran, lumbering and gasping in their fire suits, for the open pipeline hatch seventy yards away, the seething cloud of superheated, sparkling orange gas boiling after them.

Gator, who had been a step behind Roark as they approached the vent, could hear what Roark could not: the voices of Reese and Sindelar pleading through the static.

"Mike? What happened? Mike! Do you read me? What is going on down there? Reese, what are you getting?"

"Nothing, Chief. Mike? Come in, Mike."

"For God's sake, get ahold of those boys—"

Roark's back was on fire. They dived through the hatch, rolling to their feet, and lunged back together to slam the door shut. The gas hissed angrily through the crack until Roark spun the handle to seal the hatch.

They ripped off their helmets and collapsed to sitting positions on the tunnel floor, their heads between their knees, sucking for air even though all they got for breath was fetid and harsh.

"Mike? Gator? Guys, I'm beggin' you . . ."

"We're coming out," Gator radioed.

* * *

Gator hoisted himself off the ladder onto the street, followed by Roark. Reese was right there as they emerged, helping them rip off their singed suits.

Roark gestured frantically toward the hole, trying to catch his breath. "We've gotta pinch anything . . ."

"Easy, Boss, take it easy, plenty of time."

". . . Anything running through this sector! Hear me, Emmit. Water, gas, electric, whatever. Get on the horn to LAPD. Tell them they gotta clear out this park."

"Clear out the park?" Reese tugged off one of Roark's boots while Roark pulled off the other.

"Totally. And get Olber before we lose a couple of trains down there!"

"Why, Boss? What's going on? What did you see down there? The chief's going nuts."

"Whew!" Gator said, shaking his head as he tossed aside his boots. "What didn't we see?"

"I don't know," Roark said, "not exactly. A jet of gas coming out of the ground, some kind, yellow, orange, sparks shooting around inside it like lightning, hotter'n anything I've ever been in."

"He ain't lying," Gator said. "Gotta be what killed those guys. Almost got us. Can't breathe, can't see, nothin'. Like you're on fire without a fire."

"Get on the horn, Emmit." Emmit turned toward the van. "And Emmit? We'd better call Caltech, too. Get somebody who can tell me what the hell that was down there, what the hell is that yellow stuff shooting out of the rocks, stuff hot enough to kill people."

Reese trotted away. Roark and Gator looked at each other, then they both sat staring at MacArthur Park and the wide lake at its center. Flitting around in that park, oblivious, were homeless, junkies, rollerbladers, lovers, strollers. They didn't know what was beneath them. Neither did he, not really. The cops would have to sweep the park clean of people, though, until somebody knew. It seemed so unreal, now, sitting on the placid, empty city street under the warm sun and clear sky in the cool breeze.

Roark hoped like hell he wasn't overreacting and making a fool of himself. He made himself remember: seven men had died. That was real.

There wasn't a brighter, slicker new building in all of Los Angeles than the Beverly Tower, twenty pristine stories, as yet unoccupied, on the corner of Third and Vicente. A ten-foot-tall banner was strung across the facade over the elegant front doors, proclaiming: "MODELS NOW OPEN!!!"

Dr. Jaye Calder parked her green Cherokee right in front, a privileged spot always available to her, where the security guard, who always saluted her as if she were a general, could keep an eye on it. In truth, the guard kept an eye on her, too, admiring her tall, elegant beauty and long athletic legs.

She returned the salute and pushed through the gold-trimmed revolving door, strode through the majestic lobby with its copies of French antique furniture and huge mirrors, and rode the silent special elevator to the penthouse, where she fell, surprised, into the arms of Norman Calder—developer, subway-stop protester, husband.

"Here it is," he said, swinging his arm around.

The elevator had deposited her in the middle of the penthouse, which occupied the entire twentieth floor.

"Oh!" She was dumbstruck. The space had no furniture yet, no appliances. Just a beige carpet to soften her steps, and the stunning 360-degree view through glass walls over the entire city of Los Angeles. "Oh, my!"

"So . . . what do you think?"

"I . . . I'm . . ."

"Happy?"

"I think seven years ago I married a genius." She slowly strolled the perimeter of the penthouse, gazing out, shaking her head. Then she came back to him and threw her arms around him and buried her head in his shoulder. "I don't know how you did it."

"Well, three years, four banks, one hundred million dollars. But the doors are open."

"It's the most magnificent place I've ever seen. The whole building is magnificent. I'm so proud of you, honey. You never gave up."

He stroked her back. "You didn't let me."

She broke away to look some more.

"So here's how I see our future," came his voice behind her. "We move into this penthouse. You transfer to Cedars . . ."

Cedars-Sinai Hospital was just a block away on San Vicente.

". . . so you can work in a better neighborhood and be home a lot."

"Norman . . . I can't just—"

"I want you treating tennis elbows, not gunshot wounds. I hate it, that you have to go to work down there, dealing with all the junk of society."

"Are you finished?"

"Hardly. Follow me." He started toward the far end of the huge room.

She followed. "First, I'm not the condo type. You know that. It's so sterile up here, so remote, so . . . white."

"That's our whole marketing strategy." He chuckled. "For the public, at least. For you, the strategy is, we fix it up just the way you want it. Fill the place with beanbag chairs, for all I care. It's yours, ours. You don't need to save the world. This is the world, our world."

"But I'm needed at St. V's. I . . ."

He threw open the door, and the master bathroom caused her jaw to drop.

The room was the softest green from carpet to ceiling. A hot bath steamed in a long, white, clawfooted tub. No lights were turned on; illumination was from dozens of tiny altar candles. Roses and violets and lilacs filled the room with rich scents. Soft Chopin piano music came from hidden speakers. Two thick robes, one dark green, one maroon, hung behind the door.

She felt weak in the knees.

"You sounded tired on the phone," Norman said softly, putting his arms around her waist from behind, cooing into her ear, "so I took the liberty."

"Gosh, honey. Gee . . ."

He closed the door behind them.

Down in the tunnel, in the pipeline, where there was no one to see, the gas was gone, leaving—if there were light by which to see it—a yellow-orange tinge to the rusty iron walls. Along the floor were scattered dozens of blackened gray rats, swollen and split open. A subway train rumbled by in the adjacent tunnel, causing flecks of the yellow dust to dislodge and float in the dank, dark air.

When the Red Line train had passed, there was

no sound for a few minutes. Then the slightest hiss came from the small fissure in the pipeline floor, and a tiny bloom of innocent white water vapor was the only sign of life.

6
WHAT'S HOT

Dr. Rachel Wise was light-headed as she sipped her cappuccino at Starbucks and listened to Professor Alan Heim. It seemed like forever since she'd been attracted to a man. And evidently he was in a similar situation.

"I guess I've been lonely," he said.

"I guess I have, too," she found herself saying. He wasn't classically handsome—especially not with his swollen red nose—but he had such an intelligent sparkle, a gentle manner, an openness. He was quite a bit older, was the only thing. But that also probably accounted for his pleasantly mellowed ego and unfettered honesty.

"So why are you fighting me?"

"I've got to get back. The aftermath of this quake has got my boss stirred up, and—"

"Don't talk to me about aftermath!" he said, lightly touching his nose, and laughing, with her. "Were you there, at the Farmers Market?"

She fingered her cup, looking at it. "I was, actually. Actually, I was kind of hoping you'd show up. Then the quake hit, and I had to scoot back to my lab."

"So tonight, what do you say? Come on, life is short." He leaned forward and touched her fingers on her cup. "We'll do something innocent. Dinner, a walk, something like that."

"Actually, that would be lovely. Unless this whole thing about the quake gets complicated. We're getting some strange stuff. But . . . yes, let's."

On the way back to the office, she was amazed at herself. And she felt more alive than she had for years. And she couldn't wait to see him this evening.

He thought she was absolutely delightful—a woman he could spend time with, years. A woman who brought a promise for a future he had despaired of having.

Roark gnawed on a chicken-salad sandwich, feeling guilty even for eating, and sipped from a Diet Coke at his desk in the Emergency Operations Center, a bunker four floors down from street level. The phone rang four times, then he got the machine.

"Okay," he sighed to himself as he heard himself announce that they weren't home right now. Then he said, "Kel, honey? You there?"

The chattering of the jackhammers and the throaty roaring of the trucks and the scraping and screeching of the bulldozer blades continued as usual, and the trench lengthened in front of the Roark house. Added to that now was the insistent, unremitting blaring of a car horn that sounded like somebody had keeled over on the wheel.

For the first time in an hour, Kelly stopped twirling her finger in her hair and roused herself from the sofa and ambled to the window to see what was up.

The horn belonged to the black Ramcharger of their next-door neighbors, the usually patient Bosserts, Brian, the race-car mechanic, and Pam. Leaning on the horn was Pam, surrounded by bags of groceries. She had arrived home to find her driveway suddenly separated from the street by the newly extended gaping trench, which had been dug this morning after she'd left. She leaned on the horn with one hand and waggled the other one toward the driveway, trying to attract the attention of workers behind their growling, clanking machinery.

Finally a crane swung its bucket over, and two hard hats hooked onto its teeth a cable attached to one of the broad metal plates that covered finished sections of the ditch. The crane swung the plate over the gap between the driveway and street and lowered it into place, guided by the hard hats, who signaled by circling their gloved fingers as they watched the placement.

Finally the men waved Pam across, and she clapped a hand to her forehead in relief and waved back as she zipped the Ramcharger over the steel and into the safety of her asphalt drive.

For Kelly, it was the action highlight of the day so far—better than the wimpy little quake. It was a little drama that occupied at least ten minutes.

She wandered from the window and down the hall and into her father's bedroom and over to the closet. She opened the door and stared. Impulsively she grabbed a worn pair of Levi's. She went to her room and got a belt, just as the phone rang.

By the time she reached the living room, the machine had picked up. Then she heard:

"Kel, honey? You there? It's me. You must be there. Can you pick up, Kel? Huh? I'm sorry I got so busy . . ."

By now she had reached the kitchen and opened the knife drawer and taken out a big pair of scissors. Max, the dog, eyed her. "Scat!" she whispered, and Max slunk off, his long body even lower to the floor.

". . . We've got a situation down here, but I'll be back as soon as I can. . . ."

She held up a leg of the Levi's and dramatically snipped a large hole out of the knee.

". . . Disneyland's supposed to be prettier at night, anyway, so . . ."

She held up the other leg and cut a bigger hole out of that knee, then, with a flourish, swung the jeans down and stepped into them, pulled them up.

". . . if you can just hang in a bit longer, I'll see you soon."

She tightened the belt and rolled up the legs to her ankles and admired her work.

"Not soon enough," she said, smiling sardonically.

Roark finished his sandwich and tossed the bag into the trash can. He put his elbow on the desk and leaned on his hand and scanned the large maps on the walls detailing Los Angeles above and below ground. He was awaiting the arrival of Judd Haskins of SoCal Gas, a young and anxious exec whose tolerance level, on a scale of one to ten, was about a three.

Haskins stormed in just as anticipated.

"You can't do this."

"I'm not going over it with you again," Roark said. "These aren't just things I enjoy doing."

"You said you'd listen to reason. Did you actually see evidence of a rupture? Huh? I mean—"

"I said I'd listen to *new* reasons. There aren't any. Come on, I gotta check some things."

Roark walked out, Haskins nipping at his heels.

"Our switchboard looks like a pinball machine, ten thousand customers with no gas, and the temperature's going under sixty tonight!"

"Gas restored as soon as it's safe. Period. You don't want people blown up any more than I do."

"Nobody's getting blown up, Roark. What evidence do you have? I've got political clout in this town, you know."

"I know. This isn't politics. This is safety. I've got clout."

Roark poked his head in a door to see Emmit Reese at a computer bank. "Hey."

"Hey, Mike." Reese swung around on his chair. "How's it going?"

"I'm starting to miss the Mississippi."

"Mr. Roark?" His secretary waved from down the hall. "I have a call on your private line."

Kelly, at last. He hurried back to his office, leaving Haskins muttering to Reese: "Can you help me with this guy?"

He snatched the phone. "Hi, honey."

"Don't honey me."

"Oh, hi, Wendy," he said to his ex. "I thought it was Kelly. How are you?"

"The noise outside your house is driving Kelly crazy, and she hates being alone."

"I know, I know. The city's extending a storm drain—Kelly knows what's happening. She'll just have to turn up the TV, I guess. And I know she's been alone all day, but I couldn't help it. I don't like this any more than you do, or she does, but I have to be here."

"It all sounds exceedingly familiar," she said stiffly.

"Oh yeah? Familiar to me, too. In fact, hearing you yell at me gives me a *déjà vu* the size of a house."

"I'm not yelling."

"You're crabbing, same thing, just like always. Which is why I'm about to hang up. Hello?"

But the click on the phone told him she had hung up first. He slammed the receiver down. He looked up to see Emmit Reese standing in the door. "Phone just went dead all of a sudden."

Reese gave him a sympathetic smile. "I'll get a phone man out on the double."

"You got a wife that understands."

"Nobody understands today, my man."

From down the hall came the woven, undulant voices of an argument, and into view as Roark looked out of his office came Chief Engineer Stan Olber, who was once again going at it with Dr. Amy Barnes, a Caltech geology professor who Roark always thought was cuter than she generally allowed herself to be behind her disheveled look and stern demeanor. And sometimes she got a little off-the-wall.

"Maybe," Amy said, wagging a finger at Olber as they strode together in Roark's direction, "just maybe we'll continue this thoughtless underground blasting and find out if there's a fault line."

"No, no"—Olber wigwagged his hands in front of his face, looking straight ahead—"let's do it your way. Everybody goes back to horse and buggy and we empty every building over two stories tall."

"I'm not asking Stone Age! God, can't you see? I'm asking that we be reasonable."

"Reasonable your way would be not enough water, not enough transit, not enough phone lines, not enough nothin' for a population hammering us already."

"God, you just will never understand. Roark?"

"Hi," Roark said.

She stuck out her hand smartly. "I'm Amy Barnes, Caltech."

"I know. We've met." He remembered her from a talk she had given at a seminar in Reno on "Environmental Reality." He shook her hand gently, feeling a small tweak of disappointment that she didn't remember.

"Oh? Well."

"Careful, Mike," Olber said, with a gruff chuckle. "Disagree with anything she says, and you're looking at twelve months in city council hearings."

She sighed and looked away. "Would you let it go, for once." She looked at Roark. She had soft blue eyes that danced with febrile energy. "All we said was, Cahuenga's geologically unstable."

"The whole city's geologically unstable!" Olber said.

Amy flared and faced him, arms akimbo. "That's why we don't want you blowing up tunnels under it, you palooka!"

Olber put a hand on his chest and stumbled back, faking severe offense.

"Maybe you two could finish this up later," Roark suggested.

"Of course," Amy said quickly, smoothing her smock.

"Good idea," Olber said.

"Come on in and sit." He nodded to Reese, who backed out and shut the door behind them.

"Now," Roark said, sitting behind his desk and tapping his fingers together. "Amy, can you tell me what's down there?"

"Your guys didn't give me much to go on."

"I don't have much. Just the gas, the heat."

"Well, I can't say anything with certainty . . ."

Olber hid a smile.

". . . but I can tell you that only an idiot would keep a subway line open anywhere near such an event."

Roark had readied himself not to react to her aggressive style. So he just nodded. When she got wound up, she talked kind of out of the side of her mouth, which made her lips curl fetchingly.

"We ran trains through it all day," Olber said, "with no incidents."

"More of that rock-solid MTA judgment," Amy scoffed, "brought to you by the guys who collapsed Hollywood Boulevard."

"Okay, guys"—Roark held up a calming hand—"let's—"

"My engineers were down there," Olber said, unable to contain himself. "They said, 'no demonstrable risk.' That's what they said, from the scene. You got some conflicting evidence, a reason to strand all those passengers I'm responsible for, I'm all ears. Until you do, we're staying on sched"—he caught Roark's glare—"sorry, Mike."

"Amy, give me some guesses. Imagine a little bit for me. I know it's nothing you could stand behind fully. But just think aloud for me, okay? What might we have?"

"Let's take a ride."

Norman Calder accepted the salesman's unctuous invitation—the theatrical sweep of the hand, the sibilant "Yes, yes, please . . ."—and eased himself into the driver's seat of a midnight blue Jaguar XJS convertible and put his hands on the wheel.

The salesman slid into the passenger seat beside

him and, with palm out and spread fingers, gently wafted his hand in front of him from right to left, and intoned as if giving a magic incantation to the dash. "Burled wood, independent climate controls, cell phone. It's state-of-the-art."

"Beautiful," Norman said, feeling that he indeed belonged in this distinctive and sleek British roadster. With the top up and windows closed, he bathed in the aura of a leather cocoon.

"Ahem, pardon me," the salesman said, "but did I see you on the news this morning? The subway thing? Wasn't that you?"

Norman turned to him with a satisfied smile. "Yes, that was me. Opposing construction of another unnecessary subway stop."

"I can't tell you," the salesman cooed, "how good it was to hear somebody speak up like that. Protect our way of life."

"Well, thought it was my duty, you understand."

"Yes."

"May I?" Norman indicated a cassette half-inserted in the stereo deck.

"Please." The salesman put his hands together prayerfully.

Norman pushed the cassette in and sat back and closed his eyes, anticipating music.

"Hello!" the cassette announced. "And congratulations on the purchase of your new Jaguar!"

Norman looked at the salesman.

"They put the owner's manual on tape," he said,

"so you won't have to bother reading it. Also comes in compact disc."

"Aah."

Jaye strode briskly across the showroom floor from the manager's office, where she had been watching on a tiny black-and-white TV a news report showing a fairly calm evacuation of MacArthur Park. Police seemed to be quite casually cordoning off the area, and the tenor of the report was that this was to be just a brief inconvenience to accommodate an overcautious Office of Emergency Management. No big deal.

Norman pushed the switch that lowered the window. "Hi, dollface."

"You feel that?" Jaye said, her hand at her throat.

"What?"

"We just had an aftershock."

"We did?"

She indicated the chandelier, high overhead. He poked his head out the window and looked up to see the chandelier jiggling.

"Wow. Inside this Jag I didn't feel a thing. Wow." He turned to the salesman with a surprised expression. "I'll take it!"

Jaye rolled her eyes. He was so impulsive sometimes. But what could she say? He earned it, silly as it was. For her, a Cherokee made a lot more sense. She might never even drive that ostentatious car whose color reminded her of an eggplant.

*   *   *

The mobile Caltech lab was a souped-up white RV that as a civilian vehicle, Roark guessed, could sleep four or six comfortably and be lived in at ease for a month. As a lab it had more gauges and sensors and monitors and paraphernalia than he had ever seen before in so compact a space.

It was parked at the intersection of Seventh and Alvarado, the scene of the earlier disaster. MacArthur Park, evacuated and cordoned off by police tape, was now a place of eerie quiet and isolation. Dr. Rachel Wise sat hunched over a seismic map, jotting notes, logging in data.

Roark and Dr. Amy Barnes peered out a side window at the big lake in the middle of the park.

Dr. Barnes looked particularly grim. "That lake was sixty-two degrees yesterday. Today it's up to sixty-eight."

"So? It's been sunny all day."

"Mister Roark," she said stiffly, "it takes a geological event to heat a million gallons of water by six degrees in a few hours."

"An event? Heat. A hot spring, making steam down in the tunnel, heating the lake up here?"

"It wasn't pure steam in there," Amy said, narrowing her eyes as she peered out. "The sulfates on your fire suit told us that. And it wasn't a methane pocket. But there is a source of subterranean heat—and gas. More profound than you think."

"How profound?" Roark turned to face her, leaning on an elbow.

"Here's what I think. The source is profoundly deep. Maybe sixty miles. It's not just something heating groundwater that seeps down through the rock. No, it itself is following some fissure, a vertical crack in the earth."

"It itself?"

"The world sits on tectonic plates."

"Forgive me, Amy, but I know about tectonic plates. I know the Pacific Plate is sliding under the North American Plate right here in California—why we have the faults, earthquakes. Baja's headed north. I know we had a little earthquake this morning. I'm not an idiot. But please, I want to know why seven men were scorched to death down in a hole under this street."

"Are you finished, Mr. Roark?" Her voice was steady as a rock, her eyes on him steely.

"Mike. Yes. What's going on?"

"The plates sit on an ocean of molten rock, maybe fourteen hundred miles down, under tremendous pressures, and superheated gases. When the plates move, fissures can be created, escape routes for all this incredible hot power, all the way to the surface. Or, even within the plates, the incredible pressures mean the molten rock and gases are always looking for a way up—cracks, fissures, schisms, faults. Tunnels, so to speak, in the crust. On the surface, the release of sulfur can be a sign of activity, for instance. And carbon dioxide. You know about those kids they found out in the Mojave? That was carbon dioxide. You can't smell it, you can't see it."

"Hot power. Molten rock." Roark gave her a skeptical sideways glance. "Are you—"

"Lava," Rachel piped up from her seat.

Amy closed her eyes briefly. She was a bit more attuned to the requirement for delicacy when presenting what might sound like an outlandish notion.

"Lava," Roark said, pursing his lips. "Under L.A."

"There's always magma under us," Amy said, trying to moderate the effect, "as you must know."

"Yeah, way down there under the whole damn crust of the earth. But you mean on the way up."

"You have Mount Saint Helens, Lassen Peak . . . It's one of several possibilities."

"But it's the one you picked to tell me now. Mount Saint Helens, for chrissake."

She didn't answer.

"So, is there much history of that in the downtown area of Los Angeles, California?"

"Not specifically, but—"

"Paracutin," Rachel interrupted, causing their heads to snap around. "In 1943. Mexican farmer sees smoke coming out of the middle of his cornfield. A week later there's a volcano a thousand feet high. There's no history of *anything* until it happens, and then there is."

Amy sighed.

Roark nodded. "Well, thanks, guys." He swung open the door.

"Hey," Amy said, her voice less brittle now, "you invited us, remember? You asked me to imagine for you."

Roark took a step out. A few knots of people were eyeing the park here and there, police discouraging them from hanging around. All in all, OEM and LAPD and the DPW had gotten away easy so far, by giving the excuse that they'd needed to close the park temporarily to allow some emergency steam-pipe repairs. That story wouldn't hold up long, though, he knew that.

He turned back. "What do you want me to do, Dr. Barnes? Call up Olber and tell him that the 'demonstrable risk' he was looking for is lava?"

"No," she said, with a cool smile. "I'm not asking you to tell him anything. I just want enough time to do our work."

"Because the temperature in this lake went up six degrees."

"No, because seven men baked to death on a routine patch-up and nobody's come close to explaining it. To paraphrase you."

He was stung. "*Touché*," he said quietly. She was softer than she let on. Her competence was attractive. "MTA doesn't answer to the city. You know that. You know how rigid they can be. And I can't go to the mat with them unless you know something about this. You see?" He was almost pleading.

Her eyes were unwavering on his. "Then I need more than just a couple hours."

"You know the odds of that."

"You know how important it is. We've got to go *down* there, get some samples."

"That's too risky."

"For *us*, you mean. Rachel and me."

He nodded and climbed into his OEM Suburban. So far, it had been a hell of a day. He had to get back and go about trying to buy time with MTA and everybody else, and hoped he didn't look like a loony doing it. Then the whole day would be shot. Likely he wouldn't get home until after suppertime. He had to buy time with Kelly, too.

Amy leaned back against the countertop, on which seismic monitors traced their wiggly lines, and folded her arms and pinched her lips tightly together, staring out the opposite window as Roark's van disappeared down the street.

"Whatcha thinking, Doctor?" Rachel said, rocking her head slowly back and forth and rubbing the back of her neck.

Amy shook her head. "Nothing, Doctor."

"Bullshit."

"Yeah."

"We're not gonna know unless we go down there ourselves."

"Yeah."

The sun went down, casting a strange light over Los Angeles. But the strangeness was subtle, not enough to be discerned by Angelinos. It was just the gentle end of yet another sunny, mild day in the City of Angels; traffic on the freeways was winding down; palm trees rustled in the breeze that came up when the sun sank. Not much was going on. The Dodgers were in New York against the Mets. Neil Diamond—still performing, outlasting even Mick Jagger—was enchanting a crowd of aging hippies outdoors in the soft womb of the Greek Theater. Willy-Willy and Pooch were resigned to walking the streets, having been ousted by the MacArthur Park evacuation.

"What a day," Willy-Willy said. "I tell 'bout this morning? 'Stead of a quarter, a woman give me a taste of mighty fine coffee. *Fresh*. The day just went downhill."

"Could be worse," Pooch said. "Helluva nice night for the homeless."

Several miles to the west of MacArthur Park, toward Beverly Hills, it was later and darker and quieter when a lone sparrow, flushed from its nest by a raccoon, darted low over the La Brea Tar Pits.

On this night there were bubbles where there never had been before, larger than those seen by the little boy in the afternoon. When one of those bubbles popped, the hot spatter caught the wings of the sparrow, and it tumbled to the surface. It made two peep sounds before the gently undulating tar swallowed it down.

Nearby, at the edge of Hancock Park, the sidewalk looked empty. No one was walking there at this hour. No one except the ants. The last active ones of a colony were feeling their way home. There was a minute shudder in the square of paving. Just where the ants were headed, between them and their tiny granular hill, a sliver of a crack appeared. The walk was jarred, and the crack widened. It was only six inches long, an inch across. But the heat killed the ants. They simply stopped and curled up. Tar oozed out of the crack and covered them up.

7
THE FISSURE

Roark was struck by how quiet it was when he drove across the metal plates of the trench in front of his house and into his driveway. The construction machines were scattered along the trench, parked and abandoned, sleeping yellow giants. It was after 10 P.M. Kelly might be sleeping, too. Should he let her sleep? Wake her up and suffer the consequences? He had called several times, got the machine, left several messages. At least she knew he was trying. She could take care of herself. But he would have to pay a price, no matter what. Just now he was too tired to assess it.

Assuming, of course, that she was all right,

which is what he assumed without thinking about it.

He came quietly through the front door and stopped short. Confronting him on the coffee table was a fragrant mess: a bowl with a few unpopped popcorn kernels in congealed butter in the bottom; a frozen-dinner tray with all the peas remaining; a half-empty Häagen-Dazs container, half-filled with chocolate soup; five empty Diet Coke cans; a pile of bread crumbs shaped into a pyramid.

Beyond the coffee table on the sofa sat Kelly, arms folded tightly across her chest, mouth pinched, eyes shooting darts—definitely awake.

"I'm sorry, Kel." She didn't answer. "It was a crazy day." Silence. He was frozen to the spot for a moment, so forbidding was her look. "We had a real problem. It was good I went in. I was really needed."

At that her eyebrows shot up.

"Okay. I was needed here, too. I know. Try to understand. I gotta do my job, huh? That doesn't make me a bad person." He tried a small smile. "I'll make it up to you."

She released her tension. "Mom said you'd say that."

"Well, don't I always?"

"Do you ever? *Hello?*"

"Aw . . ."

"Sorry. That was over the line." She looked at her bare feet. "I hated it here. The noise drove me crazy. I hated being alone."

"Those my jeans you're wearing?"

"Yeah." Suddenly she looked sheepish, running her hands down the legs as if restoring the cuts.

He wondered if he dared tell her what went on today. No. Because he didn't really know himself. It would be like a scary rumor.

"Mom wants you to call her," Kelly said. "She doesn't care how late."

She would just want to know he was home with Kelly finally, and to berate him again for leaving her alone. He couldn't deal with that tonight.

He went to the sofa, leaned down to take Kelly's hands, and pulled her to her feet. "Come on, bedtime. Brush your teeth." He put his arm around her and guided her down the hallway. She felt so small.

"Dad? What was it today that was such a big deal?"

"Some workmen got killed, doing repairs in an underground steam pipe."

"What's that got to do with you?"

"Well, sometimes I get called, you know, when they're trying to figure out what happened in an event."

"Whatever happened about the earthquake?"

"Not much. Just precautions."

"We had an aftershock, you know."

"Yeah?"

"I dropped a plate in the kitchen."

"Did you sweep up all the pieces?"

"No pieces. I dropped it on Max's head, it just

slid off. He was like barking, you know, before it happened. Sometimes dogs know things, you know?"

"Yeah. Listen"—he gently propelled her into the bathroom— "tomorrow I'm all yours."

"I'm sorry about your jeans."

"I got plenty."

"I just wanted to be like with you, you know?"

"I know. Tomorrow."

But he was already worried about tomorrow.

Hector Solis arrived at the yard at 4:00 A.M., stoked with coffee, carrying the book *Writing Screenplays That Sell*, which had a lot of dog-eared pages. He had marked his place with a yellow legal pad, on which he made notes from time to time when he had a chance. He read for a few minutes before taking his seat at the controls. At 5:06 his Red Line #4 train picked up his first passengers of the day—eight people: four men with lunch pails, two men with briefcases, two women who might be waitresses; he liked to count the early risers as he arrived at the first station on his initial run.

As his headlights picked up the tunnel ahead of him, turning black to light and extending his vision, it was always a metaphor to him for how his life was going to go. At thirty-four, he had plenty of time, he was lean and healthy, his life was ahead of him, and would open up as steadily and dependably as did this long, winding, black tube in front of him. His screen treatment for *Subway* had taken a good turn last night, when he added to the tame soap-opera theme of the lives of people in the car around him the plot twist of finding dead repairmen on the tracks: seven men, mysteriously killed in the tunnel, their lanterns still lit.

He would sell his treatment, abandon these tunnels forever, find someone to marry, get a cabin in the San Gabriels, and write screenplays. You needed to sell only about one idea a decade to make a living. He was realistic. It was all possible. He didn't need much. He was strong. And he was always willing to work hard.

At about the same time, Hector's train had not yet reached the area of MacArthur Park, where at the corner of Seventh and Alvarado, the manhole cover was lying beside the open hole. In the predawn darkness, Drs. Barnes and Wise had removed the cover and, dressed in white coveralls but without helmets, and carrying ordinary flashlights, descended the ladder and moved off down the tunnel to the pipeline.

"Imagine working down here every day," Rachel said.

"I'd rather not," Amy said. "There's the pipeline."

They shined their lights at the huge pipe, sixty-three feet around, and then, as they arrived, focused on the hatch.

"Open Sesame!" Rachel commanded.

"We've got to turn this wheel," Amy said.

They pulled on it together, grunting with effort, until it cracked loose. Then Amy spun it around and they heard a light "whoosh" as the seal loosened in the hatch.

Carefully they stepped inside. They knew that the direction to the right was toward MacArthur Park and the area where the vent had burst. Neither was anxious to proceed down the dank tube.

"Look at all the frigging rats," Amy said, in a gagging voice.

"Split open like grilled hot dogs," Rachel said.

"Nice metaphor. Makes me feel sick. Let's go."

Amy led the way. They stepped carefully over the rats, wary that more might come darting out any second. They encountered no unusual heat, no unusual air. The concrete felt cool to the touch.

In a few minutes of inching their way along, they came to the site of the vent. Nothing was being emitted from the opening in the floor of the pipe.

"This has to be it," Amy said. She took a swipe of the wall, on her glove, some yellow residue. "This looks like sulphur. It's everywhere. Could be traces of magnesium, nickel, who knows."

"Just a crack, nothing happening," Rachel said.

"Yeah, but it's a couple of inches wide. Has to be the place. Damn!" Her flashlight flickered and dimmed.

"Batteries? I don't believe you'd come with old batteries."

"I've got others. Just annoying." She squatted to open the light, dumped the old batteries into her hand, took two others out of her jacket pocket. "Another bad day. I can feel it."

"Hard to feel like it's a good day when we're down in this hole." Rachel stepped to the crack and shined her light on it. She squatted to examine the area around the crack, looking for signs of deposits or color. She got down on her hands and knees and sniffed. She leaned her ear down close.

"Do you hear something?" Amy asked, fumbling with her batteries.

"I don't think so." She actually pressed her ear against the crack.

"I hear something."

"What?"

"I don't know. But I don't want to hear anything down here."

The moon silently lit the Mojave, eighty miles to the northeast of Los Angeles. On a Joshua tree that had arms at odd angles and bundles of cactus leaves for fists sat two turkey vultures. Their bald heads hung in repose, they faced across the shadowed ground toward where the '57 Chevy, Sun Dip's final hospice, sat half-buried in the bowl of sand.

Suddenly the vultures' beaks snapped up, their huge wings flapped, and they lifted from the tree even before the gunshot sound would have reached human ears. Then there was a rumbling in the ground, an explosive "bang," followed by a mighty crackling roar.

The ground shook. The Chevy disappeared in puffs of sand; the entire bowl sank. A crack three yards wide ripped through the declivity, gulped the Joshua tree, sliced through the desert at a zigzag pace like lightning, a raging, rending of sand and rock, a thousand bombs going off, a thousand splintering crashes in the empty desert.

In a blink, the fault was open; faster than the eye could follow, the gaping crack tore open the landscape to the southwest, toward the city of Los Angeles.

The desert echoed thunder, the air rained sulfur.

Roark sat up in bed and was thrown against the wall, then onto the floor. He staggered blindly into the hall, hearing the heavy steel plates covering the trench outside being thrown against each other. Framed family pictures fell and splintered at his feet as he stumbled toward Kelly's room, trying to get his bearings.

Kelly was sprawled half-off her bed, her face frozen in a silent scream.

"Kelly!" He grabbed her, trying to steady himself.

Now she screamed. "Dad! Dad! Dad!"

Some steel plates clanged into the excavation. Dishes smashed in the kitchen. Max howled somewhere. A living-room window imploded.

Roark hauled Kelly through this pandemonium, trying to think ahead, ripping open the front door and dashing to his pickup in the driveway.

Norman Calder was thrown on top of Jaye, then the two of them were tossed off the bed against the dresser, where for a moment the wind was knocked out of him. They were wide-eyed, gasping, terrified, confused. A bookcase toppled, pinning his legs, spewing books that covered Jaye's head.

In the attached garage, where paint cans and tools were falling and being thrown around, the alarm on the new Jaguar began to wail, and the tape cassette began to play at top volume: ". . . Chapter two, your warranty . . ."

Jaye flung books off her and struggled to her feet. Norman was still trying to get his breath. She checked him quickly.

"I'm okay, I'm okay," he said.

"Good. I've got to get to the hospital!"

She raced out to her Cherokee and sped down the dark streets, not noticing that the streetlights were out.

In the Red Line subway tunnel, Hector Solis stared ahead as his lights advanced, pushing back the blackness. To the quiet rumble of the #4 train, now approaching MacArthur Park, he imagined his plot. He could find all seven bodies at once. Or he could find one body per day for a week. They could be in the same place, or they could be scattered along his run. It was a strange alien gas that killed them, most likely. But it could have been something they ate. Or they could have been injected with an awful toxin by, say, tiny pins stuck in the soles of their boots. They would be two black men, two white men, two Hispanic men, and a—what? A woman! Yes! The motive would be: to threaten the city, hold it hostage; or to wipe out some opposition to something; or—maybe it was the most horrifying of all—a serial killer with no rhyme or reason! Yes! And only the train driver would be able to piece all this together, would recognize the—

Train #4 was yanked to a stop. Hector rocketed forward into the windshield. He was out cold, blood trickling from the top of his head, when screams came from his few early passengers. Emergency lights flickered on, flickered off, then stayed on with the dimmest light. The train sat virtually dark in the black tunnel, but the rumbling continued on, under MacArthur Park.

Amy Barnes was thrown forward to her hands and knees, her flashlight and batteries sent skittering into the blackness along the concrete floor of the pipe. For a moment she just blinked, dazed. She had fierce instincts to regain control, and she sat back on her haunches and shook her head to clear it.

"Amy!"

It was a plaintive cry, not loud.

"Rachel? Where are you? Rachel?"

Rachel's flashlight was rolling loose on the floor, and Amy crawled to it and shined it around. "Rache! Where the hell are you?"

"Amy?"

Then she saw the crack in the floor. Except that it wasn't an inch-wide crack anymore, but a fissure three feet wide. And the fingertips of Rachel's right hand, bloodless white from her desperate grip, were taloned onto the edge. Rachel screamed.

Amy scrambled to the edge and shined the light down. Rachel screamed again, scratching for a grip with her left hand.

"Here! Grab me!" Amy lay down flat and reached for Rachel's flailing hand, but missed it.

"I'm burning up!" she moaned.

The pipeline began shaking again, widening the fissure. The old concrete under Rachel's fingernails began to crumble. From down in the fissure came an explosive sound, and the deadly yellow steam shot up, engulfing Rachel and singeing Amy's face. She instinctively recoiled, then lunged again for the precipice. Rachel's white fingertips were gone. Rachel was gone.

"No, no," Amy whispered, trembling. "It can't . . ."

The hole was black. The only sounds were the rumbling and hissing of the gas.

She put her face down on the cool concrete, her fingers scratching on the concrete. But the concrete wasn't cool anymore. It was hot. She sprang up. She was confused, panicked, lonely. How could this have happened? How could this be happening? She'd never felt so out of control, so despairing. Rachel. How could this have happened to Rachel? She thought: How could I have let this happen?

A waft of sulfur odor hit her nose and snapped her head back. She had to get out. She picked up Rachel's flashlight and ran, stumbling, banging into the warming walls; to the open hatch and through it, running, breathless to the ladder, showing faintly orange in the distance from her flashlight. Under her feet the earth trembled, too.

Just after 5:30 A.M., Roark headed east on Wilshire Boulevard in the OEM van, warily crossing intersections where the stoplights were out, holding the phone with his left hand, Kelly's hand with his right, steering mainly with his knees.

"Put your seat belt on, honey," he said aside, his phone at his ear. "It's okay. Buckle up."

"How about you?"

"I'm okay. I've gotta reach around for too much stuff right now."

"I wanna call Mom. She'll worry." With shaking hands, she reached back for her seat belt and fastened it across her torso. "I hate this place."

"Soon as I'm through here. And we're going to the safest room in the city, I promise."

Finally Emmit Reese came on the line.

"What's coming in?" Roark asked.

"Power's down just about everywhere, Boss. Nine-one-one is swamped. We're lucky we got phones. They might not last either, depending."

"How about the freeway overpasses, the hospitals?"

"No reports of damage yet. It's getting light, crews will be checking the overpasses more closely."

"Even if nothing's falling down yet, everything could be weakened, of course."

"Yeah. Well, welcome to L.A."

"How'd you get in so fast, Emmit?"

"Disaster's my life, Boss. You know that."

"Take your feet off my desk." Reese laughed. "And listen, I think—"

A blast shook the van. Straight up ahead, a manhole cover soared twenty feet into the air on a jet of white steam, then tumbled back to earth and rolled wildly a few yards like a hubcap.

"Mike?"

Roark saw the second cover shoot up before he heard the blast, and this one was higher and closer. He hit the brakes, Kelly snapped forward against her harness. A third cover exploded skyward even closer, thirty yards away. He heard it clang down. Farther away, another steel plate went up. The explosions were marching right for him.

"Dad!"

"Hold on!" Roark stomped on the gas and took the exploding section like a skier on a slalom run. All the covers were blown. He slowed down. Then, abruptly, he stopped. "Jesus, will you look at that," he mumbled to himself.

"What, Dad?"

She followed his gaze off to their left. The quiet La Brea Tar Pits—Kelly called them "boring"—were smoking and seething. The nearby crack in the sidewalk where the ants had died was spewing a cloud of ash gray grit in which there were flashing red and white sparks.

"Dad?"

"Hey, Mike, you still there?"

"I'm here," he answered vaguely, agape at the scene.

"Well, don't leave me hanging here. What's going on?"

"Manhole covers, the Tar Pits, everything's— Down!"

He yanked Kelly's head down to her knees and flung himself over her, just after a blob of something a couple of feet wide, glowing red, shot out of a tar pit like a mortar shell. The blob, quickly darkening, arced over and landed with a mighty "*whump!*" just off the intersection at the base of a streetlight on Curson Avenue. The streetlight keeled over slowly and crashed on top of the boulder. A second blob was launched out of the pits and crashed on the other side of the street.

"Mike? What's that? Mike?"

"Emmit!" he yelled into the phone. "Where's the staging area nearest to Wilshire and Stanley?"

"Police or fire?"

"Fire! Underground! Huge smoke is coming out of the Tar Pits! Something like mortars or meteors, artillery shells—something is shooting out of there and bombing us! Find that geologist, Amy Barnes."

"We're calling. It's chaos over there. They're swamped. No idea where she is."

Another blob shattered the window of the Folk Art Museum, setting afire a display of devil masks. A towering billboard was hit and fell six stories. People ran out of buildings in underwear or robes.

Roark floored it again, wildly dodging the molten missiles that crashed around him, heading north on Curson. The faint dawn turned gray, the sky around him filling with what looked like ashes, falling like snow.

8
LAVA

Amy hoisted herself out of the manhole and crawled away a few yards before sitting up. She wiped her eyes and stared groggily back at the park. There were no streetlights, no traffic lights. A few silhouettes of people wandered in and out of her vision, seemingly aimless, soundless. She couldn't comprehend what had happened, couldn't even think about it.

Then she did hear something. In front of her, in the park. She shined her light in that direction.

The lake was not still. It was boiling. *Boiling*! Her mouth fell open. She fanned the light beam across the surface; steam rose all over. It was impossible. She couldn't fathom it. She couldn't *imagine* anything anymore for Mike Roark. It was all too surreal. She couldn't accept what had happened as real because it was too horrible. It was not real that Rachel was gone, not real where she'd gone.

The lights on the big board in the MTA Command Center blinked crazily, indicating locations and problems. Monitors displayed views of trains and platforms. The room crackled with dozens of radios— the voices of drivers, dispatchers, technicians. Heads bobbed to their mikes, up to the board, and swiveled to bark things to each other.

Into this hubbub at 5:42 A.M. strode Stan Olber, red-eyed, but with the crisp, commanding attitude respected by those under him. His aide, Kenny Lopez, was quickly at his side, holding his clipboard ready in front of him.

"Where we at?" Olber said, scanning the big board of lights.

"Power failures on every line," Lopez said.

"Contact with all the trains?"

"All but one. That's where our problem is."

"We got problems everywhere, I can see that, everything messed up and backed up. What's this one?"

"Red Line #4, westbound, outside MacArthur

Park." Olber winced. "We keep getting numbers that don't make any sense. Like, the onboard temperature is reading twenty degrees above normal."

"Oh Christ." Olber rubbed his eyes, remembering everything from yesterday, not wanting to believe anything.

"I'll send a crew in."

"No, no." He was sitting on a powder keg. He was sitting on too many damn crazy ideas out of the white-coats from Caltech. Whatever, he had to *sit* on it. "I'll go in myself."

Lopez looked at him questioningly.

Olber waved him off. "Go tend to business. You got plenty to do. I need all the updated information I can get. Don't worry about every little step I take."

Lopez backed off and turned away, chastised. You didn't get in Stan Olber's way, and you didn't try to read his mind. Not if you loved your job. Not if you loved your green card, which Olber helped you get.

Red Line #4 train sat in darkness in the tunnel, near where it ran under MacArthur Park. Hector tried to blink his daze away. The radio was out, evidently, because he couldn't raise anybody or hear anybody. He mopped his face with a rag, cleaning the blood off so as not to scare the passengers as he headed back into the car.

In the beam of his flashlight and the faint light from the emergency system, he saw the same eight people he'd started with, but they were no longer half-asleep. Nervous eyes turned toward him. One man flicked a lighter to check his watch.

"Douse that!" Hector commanded. "We could have ruptured gas lines around here."

The questions came at him fast and furious. "What's going on? Where are we? How long we gonna sit here? I can't breathe. Can't you *do* something?"

"Everybody cool it. Everything's under control." He felt a renewed trickle of blood by his ear, and quickly wiped it away. "Relax. Anybody hurt?"

"I can't breathe," a woman repeated.

"Why is it so hot in here?" a man asked.

"There's no fire, so don't worry about it. It always feels hot when you get stuck in a tunnel. Everybody's just gonna have to stay calm, keep from gettin' asthma. I'll take care of it. I have to go to the back. Everybody stay right where you are. We'll be up and running shortly."

The last compartment was empty. He lowered the rear window its maximum four inches. He, too, wondered why it was so hot. It was so damn hot he was having trouble breathing himself. Plus this headache. Damn radios were supposed to be state-of-the-art, just like everything else on this train. In his screenplay, he'd wrestled with whether to make the subway system look good or bad. He'd like to make it look good, but they didn't treat the drivers with much respect, to give them equipment that didn't work.

The air coming in the rear window was hotter than the air already in the car. What the hell was up with that? One thing sure, the people on his train, for whom he had responsibility while he was at the controls, were no more state-of-the-art than people ever had been, and they couldn't breathe this shit for too long without falling on their damn faces.

"Must be the hydraulics," he mumbled to himself. "Maybe I can override it."

LAPD Chief Wayne Sindelar stepped out of the elevator into the Emergency Operations center bunker—an underground complex built during the Cold War, with doors of foot-thick steel to protect against nuclear blasts—and brushed past several officials to approach Emmit Reese at the bank of computers.

"Where's your boss?" he asked gruffly.

"I expect him any minute."

"Sure," the chief said. Despite the fact that he had instituted reforms and a reorganization that had restored the LAPD to a place of national respect, Wayne Sindelar was a cynical man. He didn't trust anybody to do right or anything to go right. Nonetheless, he typically proceeded as if he himself could fix everything—or at least come closer to fixing things than anybody else. He and his department. "You know where he is?"

"He's out there somewhere being shot at."

"Shot at?"

"Red-hot stuff is spurting out of the Tar Pits and coming down like mortars. He's on his way in—if he can make it."

"*If*! He damn well better make it. We gotta get this thing coordinated!"

"I expect that's on his mind, Chief. I mean, I talked to him a few minutes ago, and he was driving like hell to get here."

Chief Sindelar clapped him on the shoulder. "That's all right. I shouldn't hammer on you. Just that he's got a way sometimes of going off half-cocked, a Lone Ranger. This is a team."

"Yes, sir, Chief. We're all in this together."

Fires lit the predawn sky. Two burning buildings lit Wilshire Boulevard where the streetlights were out. Gray ash pelted Jaye's Cherokee; her windshield wipers were under strain to clear the glass. Her eyes were riveted on the road ahead; she couldn't afford distractions; she would be needed at the hospital.

The AM radio, KNX, was staticky but understandable. The announcer seemed to be working without a script: ". . . and the metropolitan water

supply has *not*, repeat, *not* been cleared for con-
sumption. Boil everything, that's best, until we
know more. There've been reports of several fires,
and perhaps even forest fires, that are spreading
smoke and ash over the city. Best to stay home
today, that's for sure. In fact, uh, apparently a situation is developing right now in the Fairfax area. A
fire. Our Bob Rose is there, via car phone . . ."

Sirens blared behind her, and she pulled over to
allow two fire trucks to pass. A molten blob arced
high in front of her, turning black as it fell. At the
same instant she hit the brakes, the now-solid blob
hit the top of the second fire truck, which careened,
tipped up on its two left wheels, and went over,
sliding for twenty yards, sending sparks into the
already violent air over Wilshire, and sending several men tumbling along the pavement.

"Oh no." Dr. Jaye Calder aimed the Cherokee
for the sidewalk on the north side opposite the
wreck, jumped the curb, and parked it up on the
grass, out of the way of ambulances and emergency
vehicles.

On Seventh Street near Hoover, Amy wandered
the sidewalk away from MacArthur Park as confused and lost as a refugee. Her white blouse
and gray slacks, which sweat had plastered to
her body under the white coveralls, were still

matted. Her short dark hair went every which way, punkish. Her hands were grimy, her finger-nails jagged.

She passed a hardware store whose window had been shattered, and was oblivious to the looters jumping in and out. The fireworks in the sky didn't distract her. But, while dazed and exhausted, mentally and physically, she was neither lost nor confused. She had a mission.

She got to the Humvee—the squat, Army-designed, four-wheel-drive, field-research vehicle they had come in—and leaned against it. Facing west, she saw the ominous cloud that stiffened her.

Even in these dark pre-dawn hours it was visible. The growing ash cloud over the tar pits was shimmering with electricity, glowing, tumbling.

Amy crawled into the Humvee and headed right for the glimmering cloud.

Roark had stopped the van when he felt he was more or less out of range of most of the missiles that crashed down from the general direction of Hancock Park. Still, Kelly scanned the dark sky as if looking for UFOs, while her father crawled around the back of the van, ripping into emergency packets of gauze, salve, tape, antibiotic ointments, getting them ready for quick access.

Over the police scanner came the call:

"Seventeen is down! Fire engine seventeen has turned over! Wilshire at Stanley! We've got casualties!"

Right at Hancock Park. "Okay, Kelly." Roark scrambled back into the driver's seat. "Hold on, we got a stop to make."

The fire truck lay on its left side, its driver trapped inside. Low moans came from some of the other five firefighters lying scattered on the asphalt. Jaye knelt on one knee in a patch of blood over the man who appeared to have the most serious head injuries. She applied pressure to the side of his head with a beach towel from her car. Nearby, a man in a white warm-up suit, now spattered with blood, comforted a firefighter whose leg was broken and lay at an odd angle.

"Easy, take it easy," Professor Heim said, wincing at the sight of white bone jutting out from bloody tissue, "and lie still. You got a compound fracture. Hold on. Help is coming."

"Oh my God it hurts," the man moaned. "Sorry to be such a baby. You're bleeding, too."

"My nose was busted before. Doesn't even hurt."

"My buddies . . ."

"Everybody's being taken care of. Lie still."

A hundred yards farther on, some of the men from the lead fire truck were already deployed, aiming their hoses at the seething cauldron which was the La Brea Tar Pits, cursing the lack of effect of the water streams and ducking to avoid globs of spattering tar. Two of their cohorts had run back to tend to their wounded comrades from the second truck, and had quickly set up emergency halogen lights on tripods, which lit up the immediate scene like day.

Roark eased the van to a stop across the wide boulevard from the wrecked truck and quickly assessed the scene. He heard sirens all over.

"Stay right here," he said to Kelly, who was wide-eyed and still trembling, but frozen in place. "Don't move. I'll be right out here."

He stepped out and was bumped by the fender of a green Saab that was fortunately coming to a stop. In the Saab was Bob Rose, the KNX reporter, who, ogling the scene and talking eagerly into his car phone, was oblivious to Roark.

"Get outta here!" Roark bellowed.

Rose was broadcasting: ". . . I'm now in front of the La Brea Tar Pits, where fire trucks have responded to reports of gunfire, and we have here an overturned—"

Roark slammed his hand down on the fender and Rose flinched so hard the phone popped out of his hand and clacked against the windshield.

"Beat it, you jerk!" Roark hollered.

Without waiting for the result, he trotted across the street to where Jaye knelt. "Ambulances will be coming, ma'am," he said, touching her shoulder. "Maybe you should let—"

"I'm a doctor," she said, not looking up. "This man may have a skull fracture."

"Okay. Thanks."

Roark turned toward the truck, where he heard somebody yell, "Get him outta there!"

He joined a fireman climbing up the chassis to reach the passenger side, which was on top.

The truck shook. "Aftershock!" Roark said. They held on. The shaking became more violent, the tipped truck shifted. There were cries from the fire-fighters up ahead.

When Roark looked, he was rocked again by what he saw.

Amid the Tar Pits appeared an orange-red molten glow, and under it, pushing it slowly up like phantasmic sunrise, was a stubby black cone at first the size of a fireplug, then widening at its base as it inched up. The glow began sliding off the top, became a tongue of bubbling, seething, fiery orange ooze a yard across, spreading, reaching for the street.

There was a moment when all viewers were too stunned to move. Roark silently mouthed, "Lava." The lava tongue moved slowly, fitfully, as the tip would darken and slow, to be overridden by a small surge behind it, again and again, forming small pillows as it advanced. Its glow eliminating the darkness, the lava slid around a telephone pole, engulfing the base; the pole wiggled, wavered, and toppled into the hellish goo, instantly consumed in flash flame.

Then everybody was yelling and running at once, a helter-skelter escape from an incomprehensible pursuer. Car doors slammed, tires screeched, fenders banged. Roark watched, riveted to his perch on the overturned truck as the lava slid over the curb and onto Wilshire Boulevard, fanned out across the pavement ten feet wide to maybe a six-inch depth, and kept coming, faster now, heading west, toward the truck. Firefighters bravely backed up, still keeping their hoses trained on the advancing lava, even though the water was tossed off the back of the flow instantly as ineffectual steam. Roark could only gaze dumbly, a deer in headlights, as the lava approached the wreck. Until he heard Kelly scream.

The van! He had forgotten the van was across the street from the truck, and Kelly was screaming behind closed windows. The lava had reached them, would soon lick at the vehicles, would flow between them, and he saw her wrestling with the seat belt, then flinging the passenger door open and leaping out to the sidewalk on the north side of the street.

Roark jumped down to his side, and he and Kelly locked eyes from across the great divide, on opposite sides of the boulevard, as the leading edge of the lava began to slide between them, touching the front of the Suburban. He dashed across the street, behind the Suburban, feeling the heat from the slowly advancing tide. He heard tires pop on his van, saw it sink to the pavement, at the same time that a molten blob whistled through the air and plopped to the sidewalk a few feet from Kelly, where it sizzled, then spat a fleck of lava to the side.

The fleck landed on Kelly's leg, setting fire to her jeans. "Dad!"

He reached her, wrenched off her jacket, used the jacket to smother the flame. But the jeans had burned through, her leg was singed, and she whimpered with pain as she leaned against him. He picked her up. The sky darkened. Ash snowed on them, and she choked as it dusted her face.

Roark looked frantically around. Lava was consuming the Suburban, from the bottom; the vehicle slowly sank into the oozing stream, bursting into fire. A scream came from the overturned fire truck. A firefighter had climbed up, pried open the passenger door, and lowered himself inside to get to the pinned driver. Another crewman had climbed up behind him and was prepared to pull them both out. But lava had reached the cab, and both the firefighters inside were now trapped, being burned alive. Other crewmen had to forcibly pull the third man down from the cab, as he moaned and tried to wrestle free to save his buddies. "Too late!" they yelled at him. "Too late! Give it up!"

The lava flow, still rather shallow, only a few inches deep, seemed to be confined to the roadbed, as if led down Wilshire. Ahead of it now, Roark saw the doctor he had first encountered with the head-wounded fireman, her arms under his shoulders, trying to drag him out of the path.

There was a bus bench behind Roark, and he laid Kelly down there, with closed eyes, still whimpering. She would be safe, out of the path of the fiery stuff. He ran into the street and grabbed the legs of the wounded man, and together with the doctor moved him off the street to the bench beside Kelly.

Roark ran back into the street, this time to the fireman with the broken leg, and, helped by the civilian in running clothes, took the man, who was weeping with pain, back to the bench.

"You okay?" Roark asked Alan Heim.

"Yeah. This all from the damn earthquake?"

"Don't see how. Don't know."

After they placed the firefighter down, Heim ran for his bicycle, thinking: *I've gotta call Rachel. She'll know.*

Roark knelt with the doctor beside their three casualties as the lava continued down the street beyond them.

"Jaye," she said, raising her voice above the din, sticking out her hand quickly.

"Mike," he answered, shaking it briefly.

"We have to get these people to a hospital. Best one near here is Cedars. I'll take them."

"Yeah. This is my daughter. I'll take her myself."

"You're OEM, right?" He nodded. "You're needed here. I'll take her, all of them."

"I don't—"

"Let me take her to Cedars. That's a second-degree burn. It'll be okay, but it could get infected if we don't deal with it."

Tires exploded, vehicles sagged and melted, power lines fell and crackled, alarms and sirens wailed. From time to time, clouds of ash blew over. The lava reached the row of palm trees lining the entrance to the Los Angeles County Museum of Art, and one by one the trees tipped and fell, their fronds waving until they were incinerated.

Roark looked at Kelly, who grimaced in pain with eyes closed, and back to Jaye. "Okay. Take her."

"Dad?" she said feebly.

"It's okay, hon. Dr. Jaye's gonna take you. You'll be fine."

"Are we going home?"

"To the hospital, Kel. I'll be there in a sec."

They carried her to the Cherokee, then the wounded, groaning firefighters, whom they laid in the back.

"She allergic to anything?" Jaye asked, panting.

"No, don't think so."

Jaye pulled a business card out of her pocket and slapped it into Roark's hand. "My page number's on it."

"Dad, who is this lady?"

"The doctor, Kel. She'll take care of your leg." He rubbed her brow.

"I don't want her to. Can't I stay, Dad? I won't be in the way."

"No, it's not safe for you here. I'll be with you very soon."

"My leg really hurts."

"She'll fix the pain, in just a second." He backed away and closed the door. "Go, Doc!"

"Dad, no! Let me outta here! Dad!"

He heard her yelling as Jaye sped away down the stretch of grass to get ahead of the lava, and it wounded him more than he'd ever remembered being hurt.

9
FLIGHT

The retreating firefighters kept their hoses trained on the advancing lip of lava as it moved west on Wilshire Boulevard, deeper now, maybe a foot, all emanating from the low cone in the Tar Pits, from which slid a steady stream. Spotlights crisscrossed the ground and sky as if there were an air raid.

Roark needed a radio. He trotted toward the Folk Art Museum at the other end of the park, where a Fire Department emergency vehicle was parked in the driveway, and a captain was on the radio.

"Request additional units and paramedic support," the captain was saying.

Roark waited behind him. When the captain glanced around, Roark motioned to the radio. "I'm Roark," he said.

The captain nodded, signed off, handed Roark the mike. He wanted to contact Emmit Reese at the EOC bunker, but LAPD Chief Sindelar intercepted the communication and took the mike himself.

"Roark! Where the hell—"

"I'm at the scene on Wilshire." He had to holler. "Just listen. We need a declaration of emergency and immediate assistance from county, state, and federal, plus all National Guard units available. We need them right here. And I need every K-Rail concrete barricade and divider available anywhere. Contact the highway people. Got it?"

"Roger. Cal-Trans is checking overpasses right now. Everything we're getting here is pretty sketchy, Roark."

"Wayne, we're at *level one* here. Now listen. Public Works has some equipment close by that we can use—from the Hollyhills trench. Jackhammers, skiploaders, dozers—I need it all."

"Where's it at on the trench?" Sindelar was jotting notes.

"Crescent Heights, north of Pico. Right outside my door is a good place to look. They're also digging up Sunset at San Vicente. We gotta have every rig there is."

"Okay, Roark. Just get in here. This place is a

mess, chickens with heads cut off. We gotta coordinate from here; otherwise, we're flying blind while you bang around out in the boonies."

"Ten-four."

Roark handed the radio to the captain, wishing he had a direct line to Cedars.

Jaye sped toward Cedars-Sinai Medical Center, glancing occasionally at the fireman slumped beside her, blood from his head-wound staining through the towel.

"I think you should pull over," Kelly said from the back seat, looking at the fireman groaning in pain beside her. "This guy's leg is gushing."

"There's a blanket under him," Jaye said calmly. "Pull it out, and press it down over the wound, hard."

"I can't," Kelly shrank away. "I think you have to—"

"I can't argue with you, Kelly. If we don't get to the hospital, I might lose *both* of these guys. You have to help me now."

"I want my Dad here with me."

"Yeah? I'd like a team of nurses and an operating table, too. What I've got is you. We're both scared. So Kelly, I drive, you press that blanket on his wound. Do it now."

"My leg still hurts."

"I know. Hang in, little lady. You gotta be as tough as that poor guy beside you."

Kelly gave a small whimper and reached for the blanket.

Roark saw Amy Barnes step out of the Humvee and come walking over, looking dirty and dazed.

"You were right," was the first thing he blurted.

"No."

"What happened to you?" he asked, looking her up and down, and taking her arm to lead her toward the museum building, farther away from the flaming stream on Wilshire.

"Rachel's dead."

"*Dead*? How?"

"She fell into the fissure." Her voice was flat, her eyes dull. "You see, the crack in the pipe, it was this." She swept her arm slowly around to take in the scene. "The earthquake, the fissure, the crack in the pipe. We have a magma chamber somewhere deep underneath. Up here we have a volcano."

"Was that it? In the Tar Pits? A real volcano?"

"How big it'll get, how long this will go on, we can't know," she went on in a monotone. "The lava is flowing pretty fast, but it's not exploding out of the cone as it could. It's just sort of oozing out, like Mauna Loa. We have some ash, but it could be worse. The ash could be bigger—it's granulated rock pieces, you know, not real ash like from burned wood."

Dr. Amy Barnes (Anne Heche) is all smiles before the volcano begins to wreak its havoc.

Lorey Sebastian

Seismologist Rachel Wise (Laurie Lathem) hangs on for dear life.

Lorey Sebastian

Gaby Hoffman as Kelly Roark.
Lorey Sebastian

A panicked Dr. Amy Barnes (Anne Heche) is showered with ash.
Lorey Sebastian

Stan Olber (John Carroll Lynch) rescues the driver of a trapped MTA subway.
Lorey Sebastian

A fire engine, useless against the tide of lava, is engulfed in flames.

Mark Fellman

Dr. Jaye Calder (Jacqueline Kim) treats an explosion victim.

Lorey Sebastian

Dr. Amy Barnes, seismologist (Anne Heche).
Lorey Sebastian

Dr. Jaye Calder (Jacqueline Kim), dedicated surgeon.
Lorey Sebastian

Uncontrollable fires on the streets of L.A.
Lorey Sebastian

"But what are these damn blobs sailing around?" Just as he asked, one hit a building down the street, setting it afire.

"Those are lava bombs. Sometimes rocks and pieces of rocks are just exploded out with steam and gases—varying sizes of fragments down to what we call ash, and they can go miles up. But sometimes what's exploded out is what you call 'blobs' of molten rock. That's what these are. Molten rock that solidifies fast as it cools in flight or when it lands."

"Lava bombs." Roark was dumbfounded by the whole unmanageable situation, but tried to retain concentration on the immediate matter at hand. "What do we do?"

"You can't put a plug in it." Amy gave a silly giggle.

"Come on, Amy!" He took her shoulders and shook them.

She seemed to come awake, blinking.

"I need your help," he said, peering into her eyes.

The fire captain strode by, a section of hose over his shoulder. "We need some traffic blocks at Fairfax," he called to Roark. "It's outta control."

"How do we funnel it out of here?"

"Just stop it. My men have to have room to work."

"But all the cars have to—"

"Just get that traffic blocked!" the captain said fiercely, striding on.

Roark turned back to Amy, whose eyes now looked more alert. "I've got K-Rails coming in, to try to keep this stuff moving in a corridor down Wilshire, off the side streets. What do you think?"

"It's lava."

He shook her shoulders again, this time more gently. "We're gonna dig up the streets, build some berms along the edges. What else should we do, Amy? What else?"

"If I were you," she said evenly, meeting his gaze, "I'd evacuate the Westside."

"The *Westside*! Are you *nuts*? The ritziest part of the city? You know what they'd do to me?"

"You're worried about where the *money* is? You're worried about ritzy houses and ritzy shops and ritzy attitudes? This is *lava*, Roark, I'm trying to tell you. You can't *zone* it into another neighborhood. You can't treat it like a river. And you can't really fight it either."

"What are you saying? Just surrender the Westside?"

She squirmed out of his grip, took a step away, then faced him. "You might have to surrender the whole damn city, damn you! Don't you hear me? Don't you know what this thing is? You know what a *volcano* is? A volcano does what it wants to do. The lava goes where it wants to go. All we can do is get out of its way and hope it doesn't go all at once."

"Where's it going? How can we tell what the

hell it's going to do and where the hell it's going?"

"You can't tell much. It's heavy stuff, goes downhill. But we don't know what's down under that cone. We don't know where the magma chamber is or how big it is. We don't know if there's gases or groundwater about to blow. We don't know if the cone might shoot off straight up, or the whole damn side of the thing might go out horizontally. We don't know if another quake will split it open and let the ejecta just spew out everywhere. It could run out of energy in a day. Or it could go on for years. Fast or slow. If it blows, everything you see around here will be gone. We have to get out of its way."

"So you still don't *know* much."

"I know it's a volcano. The rest is a judgment call."

The lava rolled up over the curb for a stretch along Wilshire. It reached a bus stop, melting the plastic shelter so that its graffiti letters elongated into weird shapes; the bench ignited into a brief, crackling blaze and was gone.

"Your judgment."

"If you'd have listened to my judgment yesterday, you might have been better prepared."

"Yeah, okay, okay."

Over the sirens, he heard a car horn and looked up to see Gator Harris in his red-and-white '75 Ford Torino.

"Yo, Mike!" Gator waved.

Roark went over and leaned in. "You're a trouper, Gator."

"I ain't fireproof. Let's get outta here. They sent me after you."

"I figured. I need you here, Gator. Cedars is gonna be swamped. I want you on point over there."

Gator flinched and snapped his head around as, down the street, a bridal-wear shop flashed into flame, its plate-glass windows crashed, and lava rolled in. Mannequins of bride in gown and groom in tux drooped, melted, burned.

"I got a better idea, Boss," Gator said. "How about you and me and the mad scientist over there head on back to the EOC? You got a desk. That's where you work."

Roark shook his head and looked away. "Can't do it, Gator."

"They told me not to take a no."

"Kelly's at Cedars."

"Your daughter?"

"Burned leg. Doctor named Calder brought her in, a woman."

Gator pursed his lips and nodded, tapping his wheel with his big hand. "I see. Okay. She'll have a private suite by noon."

Roark clapped him on the shoulder. "See you over there."

Gator revved the engine, staring ahead. "Chief, we gonna be okay, this city?"

"I hope so. I don't know. Nobody knows."

Just before 6 A.M., a short way along Wilshire, just beyond the museum and the corner of Hancock Park, the lava found Ogden Drive on the south side, and some of it slid off that way, into the residential neighborhood. A cloud of ash blew in. Choking, gasping, yelling residents grabbed clothes, kids, pets, wallets, and dashed frantically down walks, across lawns, their faces reflecting the mad glow of the thickening lava tongue that now reached for the very cars toward which they fled. Some turned away and ran back. Some reached their cars and wheeled into wild screeching spins and crashes, nobody knowing which was now the way out.

"Mitch! Mitch!" yelled one panicked woman, waving wildly at a man who had jumped into a car and was grinding and grinding the starter. "Wait, Mitch!"

She heard the "thunk . . . thunk . . . thunk . . . thunk" as all four tires went down and the car sank into the lava amid sparks and gurgles, and she heard Mitch yowling as fire consumed the entire insides, and the charred shell was carried along in the molten muck like a cork toy.

Two blocks farther on at Wilshire's intersection with Fairfax Avenue, seven firemen tore at the street with jackhammers, their coats and hats off, sweat pouring down their bodies.

"Whew!" said one, stopping to mop his brow. As if on cue, the others stopped to wipe their faces. "We need backhoes. Where the hell are they?"

"Supposed to be coming," one answered.

"Forget backhoes," another said. "You can probably just as well forget jackhammers." He gestured east down Wilshire Boulevard.

Two blocks away came the lava, grinding and flashing. As successive sections overflowed the cooling and slowing ones at the lead, hulks of cars, kiosks, garbage cans, trees, and signs tumbled slowly with the molten rock.

"Hit it, guys!" The men leaned urgently on their clanking jackhammers again, breaking up the pavement.

A few minutes later, as the lava edged closer, three fire trucks arrived at the intersection, and ladders went up the side of Johnnie's Coffee Shop. Crews ran up with hoses, clambered onto the roof, and stood poised to turn their streams on the flow when the call came. Scores of cars lined up at the intersection on Fairfax kept up a constant din of honking, but the officers were letting them through just a few at a time, to allow the firemen to do their work.

Now and then a helicopter thumped overhead. Flight restrictions had been put on the area, and very few were allowed in the air. But police choppers were up, and one for the TV pool coverage, and a few others ferrying emergency personnel. But nobody could land anywhere near the action, and most pilots just returned to their pads, landed, and put their machines away.

A fierce argument was going on around the corner—one that on any other day would have stopped passersby, drawn the curious to windows:

"Whaddaya mean, you can't get me any barricades!" hollered LAPD lieutenant Bert Fox.

"You got ears?" hollered back Murray Levy of Cal-Trans. "I said I can't." He cupped his hands over his mouth and leaned close to Lieutenant Fox's face. "I can't because I can't get any *cranes* to lift the bastards!"

"Easy, guys," Roark said, pacing a few yards away.

"Since when can't you get cranes? You got no *organization*! That's what."

"The trucks are all in the *valley*, you numskull! You can't just pull a gun on a truck and say, 'Go pick up a crane!'"

"Okay, okay." Roark stepped between them, then faced Levy. "How many *can* you get me?"

Levy shrugged.

"Can you get me *any*?"

"I'm working on it."

"Work harder, Levy," Roark said, staring hard. "You never had a more serious job to do."

His cell phone jangled in his pocket, and he took it out to answer it.

Meanwhile, across the intersection, Amy Barnes was looking through the shattered display window of a May Company store. Her eyes went over the scattering of athletic gear, including footballs, baseballs, and a basketball. She stepped into the window and picked up the basketball and rolled it around in her hands. "Yes," she said, as if to say to a salesperson, "I'll take it."

Victims filled the hospital and overflowed it. Even Gracie Allen Drive, which runs under the middle of Cedars-Sinai Medical Center, was now an outdoor emergency room; dazed patients sat or lay on gurneys, some of them bandaged, some just bloody. Some were unconscious. The patients, not active themselves, were the center of frantic action. Doctors, nurses, paramedics, interns darted around, bending over the gurneys, sprinting in and out of the hospital, stethoscopes flopping around necks. Sirens of arriving ambulances were incessant, almost irrelevant: every vehicle was an emergency vehicle on a call.

"Got a cardiac arrest here!" Dr. Jaye Calder

shouted, her hand on a patient's chest. "Seventy-five milligrams of Lidocaine, stat!"

Gator sat at the curb, next to a stretcher, holding a cell phone tight to his ear, covering the other ear with his hand to hear better. Kelly was on the stretcher, watching Gator.

"How is she?" Roark asked.

"Dr. Calder says she'll be fine." Gator tried to sound light and easy.

"I want to talk to her."

Gator handed the phone to Kelly.

"Hi, Dad. I'm okay. My leg doesn't hurt so much. Are you coming here?"

"I can't just yet, sweetheart. Things are kind of crazy out here. You sure you're okay?"

"I'm just resting for a while. But I can walk around. There are some little kids around here, and Dr. Jaye said she may need me to baby-sit them."

"You're terrific. I love you. Let me talk to Gator."

"Aw—" Kelly slowly handed the phone back to Gator.

"Chief, you've gotta stop sending bodies this way. We got a full house over here. Patients all over the place, outside even. Not just earthquakes, but we got car accidents, burns, smoke inhalation. They're doing triage on the damn sidewalk!"

"Cedars is the only place close that's north of the flow!" Roark hollered. The pounding of the jackhammers and honking of horns and blaring of sirens made it almost impossible to hear. "If I send somebody to block off traffic on Third, can you put the postops in the Beverly Center—they got a ton of room."

"I'd bet on it."

"Okay. Have Emmit dispatch it. Stay there until it's up and running."

"You got it."

"And Gator?"

"Yeah?"

"She really look okay?"

"Prettiest thing I ever saw lying on a curb during a volcano."

"Gator, listen to me. Don't let her out of your sight. You gotta promise me!"

"Hey, this is Gator you're talking to. I gotta promise you to do what you know I'm gonna do?"

"I'm glad you're there, Gator."

"Me, too."

"Jesus, here comes the big stuff. Talk to you later."

"Roger, Chief. Ten-four."

Loaders, tractors, dozers rumbled toward the intersection from the east, a parade of yellow equipment such as had been working on the trench outside Roark's house. A Public Works truck with flashing yellow lights on the roof led the way.

As he watched the approaching procession, Roark saw Amy walk into the intersection carrying a basketball. He watched, puzzled, as she carefully put the basketball down, took her hands off the ball, and straightened up. The ball began to roll slowly to the south, toward Fairfax. It rolled under the line of honking cars, gathering speed, and disappeared.

Roark got it: the street banked slightly to the south. Amy was looking for a tiny edge in confronting the lava; knowing where it might go was an edge, where gravity might pull it. That meant that there was a special problem, though, with those cars.

The parade of heavy equipment reached the intersection. The man driving the leading pickup got out and ambled over to Roark, carrying his hard hat with one hand, running his other hand over his blond crew cut, his wide eyes focused down the boulevard at the glowing lava, now a block away.

"You Porter, the supervisor?" Roark asked.

"You Roark?"

"Yeah. Listen. We gotta slow this thing down. A trench, berm, whatever you can give me. Move anything you want, dig anything you want. Okay?" He grabbed the arm of LAPD Lieutenant Fox, who was hurrying by. "Lieutenant, all the traffic on Fairfax has to be turned around *now*."

"Why?"

"I don't think the flow's gonna hold its present line. See, it's heavy stuff, and any slight—"

"Hang on a second," Supervisor Porter interrupted, sticking a hand between Roark and Fox, spitting off to the side and gazing down the street. "I'm pulling my crew out."

Fox and Roark looked at each other, then at Porter.

"Beg pardon?" Roark said.

"This ain't our kind of job. Way too hairy. It's Fire Department all the way." He spat again and folded his arms across his chest.

"Now, wait a second—" Fox began.

"Fire Department doesn't have the equipment, Porter," Roark said sternly. "You do."

"Nope. No protective gear. No special training. Insurance is iffy. I'm responsible for the safety of my guys. Nope, this is no good."

Lieutenant Fox thrust his chest at Porter. "You got a duty as a public servant."

"Public Works, Lieutenant. Not the marines."

"Leave everything," Roark said abruptly. "All the equipment."

"Leave it?"

"We'll get people to run it."

"*My* machines? You gonna get amateurs to run machines? You gonna get amateurs to run *my* machines?"

"You gonna run 'em?"

"No, but—"

"Then we'll run 'em."

"You gonna sign for this stuff?"

"Beat it, Porter."

Porter shrugged, turned, stuffed his hands in his trouser pockets, and, as casually as he could manage with Roark and lava a couple of hundred yards behind his back, walked away.

All at once the fire hoses came on, hard streams from the men on the shop roofs shooting over the street to hiss against the leading edge of the tumbling lava. Occasionally a hunk would seem to darken and slow, but then fresh orange lava would burst out around it and forge ahead.

The lava was at the intersection. Public Works drivers spilled out of their rigs and headed for the side streets. The flow reached the first heavy-equipment rigs, hissing and sparking, shooting up rays of flame as it contacted the paint and steel.

A momentary hush fell over the intersection, as awed motorists in a hundred cars in the blocked line on Fairfax dropped their hands from their horns to gape at the spectacular confrontation: the incredible, unstoppable force of nature against unmanned mechanical beasts.

But then jaws dropped farther as the lava flow began to split. Part of it continued in among the wheels and treads of the machines. The fire hoses from the rooftops continued to pour on that. The other, larger part slid off to the left, turning like a glowing serpent, and crept toward Fairfax, directly at the line of cars.

Lieutenant Fox gaped. "What the hell—"

"It's following the slope," Roark said grimly. "Gravity is taking it downhill, toward the ocean."

The lava that had come west on Wilshire was now slithering south on Fairfax, a diabolical turn into the traffic that was already waiting to flee the area, and the resulting mash was loud and lethal.

Trapped drivers panicked. Cars backed, bucked, crashed, turned, screeched. Doors were thrown open as drivers leaped out and fled back down the street. Some, darting in among the vehicles, were caught and crushed in the spasm of movement. Some still standing screamed when their legs were caught between bumpers.

Adding to the melee was a National Guard truck, loaded with men dispatched to the scene to help control traffic, that was speeding up Fairfax at the same time, right into the teeth of the jam, and had to careen up onto the sidewalk to skid sideways to a stop.

"Close enough!" yelled the sergeant, springing from the cab in full battle gear. "Everybody out! Let's clean this mess up!" Only then did he recognize the full threat of the lava. "Holy Moly!" He waved the men to disperse. "On your toes, soldiers! Don't step in anything!"

From a spot a few yards north of the intersection

on Fairfax, Lieutenant Fox watched wearily as the lava that had eaten off the fronts of the bridal shop and coffee shop in these blocks of Wilshire now turned its awful, ineluctable molten appetite into a new venue. A squad car whined to a stop, two wheels on the sidewalk, and officers McVie and Jasper, who just yesterday had had the tamer job of dealing with the auto accident over at the A.M.E. church, got out, today wearing street clothes.

"Where the hell you been!" Fox growled. The officers were, as usual, silent under his glare. "I want you ahead of the flow. Neighborhood control. Go!"

Officer Jasper gaped across the intersection and pointed, looking questioningly at his lieutenant.

"Yes, *there*! Get down there pronto, or I'll have your asses *and* your badges!"

Officer Jasper's mouth silently formed the question, "How?"

"Find your way, dammit!"

Lieutenant Fox headed over to Roark and the freeway expert, Murray Levy of Cal-Trans. All three were shaking their heads. "We're not staying ahead of this," he said.

"What's south of us?" Roark asked.

"Down there? Convalescent home. There's a gas station."

Roark sighed through clenched teeth.

"We need the feds," Levy said.

"We got a Guard unit."

"I mean, *everybody*. I mean, they call everybody up for a hurricane. Of course, that's in the *East*, where they get *all* the federal attention."

"This is just Day One. The office is in touch."

"When are we getting those goddamn K-Rail dividers?" Fox said.

"Working on it."

"Oh, for chrissake! We got lava, you guys move like molasses!"

10
FIGHTING BACK

Twenty feet underground, but in fact not far from all the hullabaloo on the surface, the Red Line subway tube was dark and hotter than Death Valley. Stan Olber, unaware of the action above, led a crew of ten sweat-drenched, heavy-breathing men, all carrying oxygen tanks, crowbars, and first-aid packets, down the tunnel toward the area under MacArthur Park.

Finally their halogen beams picked up their quarry. "Here we go," Olber said, as the lights focused on the rear of the #4 train.

Drops of sweat flicked off them as they began to trot toward the dark train.

Olber climbed up and pried open the rear door

and flashed his light inside. "Oh Jesus. . . We got casualties!"

They followed him in. Olber reached the first man and squatted to feel his carotid artery just under his jaw. "I've got a pulse here."

The crew spread out to the fallen passengers, echoed his findings. "Got one here, too." "Yup, this one's breathin'." "I got a pulse."

"Let's get these people to the station floor," Olber directed.

"Hey, Stan?" came a voice from outside the rear door."

"Whatcha got, Pete?"

"Come here."

Olber climbed down. Pete was on all fours, pointing under the train. Olber knelt with him.

"Uh-oh," Olber said softly.

What they saw was lava. A flow was heading at them down the tunnel, already at the front of the train, not deep but as wide as the tunnel. It hissed as it reached the steel car.

Olber sprang up and hollered, "Every one of these bodies off the train! Now! We got molten lava under the train!"

They helped each other hoist the unconscious passengers up onto each other's backs. A couple of the fallen men were rotund, and Olber's crew struggled to get them slung up with their arms dangling over the front, where the carrying crewman, bent under the weight, could hold them for the climb down and the trip a hundred yards back up the tracks to the station platform.

As lava melted the undercarriage in the front, the lead compartment sank. Olber started forward.

"Where you going?" Pete said, lifting the last passenger.

"Driver."

"No time! He might not even be there, Stan!"

"He's there. He wouldn't desert his passengers. Get these people back to the station."

The floor under his feet as he hurried forward felt on fire; the train was sloping more in the direction he was headed. The door to the cab was open. Flames licked at the windshield. The entire cab was tipping forward, the walls distorted as if made of melting wax. Hector Solis was slumped over his controls, his right hand still holding a wrench clamped onto a valve.

Olber pried his fingers off the wrench, hauled him up, and tossed the slender man over his shoulder like a bag of wheat—grateful that the driver was so slight, not because it made it easier, but because his lightness made it possible for Olber to carry him at all through this sapping heat. He headed back to the rear compartment—a severe uphill climb by now—feeling burning on the soles of his feet, and his hands and shoulders so wet with sweat that he could hardly keep a grip on the limp form of Hector Solis. He came to the last compartment. He was relieved to see that everybody else was gone. The place was as hot and lonely as hell.

Hollis was propped up on three silk pillows, with an earphone plugged into her ear from her white Sony radio. The plush bedroom still showed signs of the earthquake the day before: a hairline crack zigzagging down the far wall; a broken hand mirror on her lavender vanity.

She knitted her hands together. "Jim, it's moving south. Thank God, it's moving south."

"We're moving south?" he asked dazedly, barely awake, his face buried in his pillow.

"The *lava*, dear. We're safe. Martinique can come and clean after all today. And make some *coffee*, at last. Did I tell you, dear, at the subway protest yesterday, a man actually came up to me and *begged*. Fortunately, I had some Starbucks mocha java with me. You see what happens to a neighborhood when they add a subway? It's dreadful."

"The lava?"

"Haven't you heard anything this morning? We're having a *lava* flow, dear, on Wilshire. But it's gone south."

"Good."

*   *   *

The flow on Curson was not as big as the original on Wilshire or the part of that that had turned onto Fairfax. But the dead-end street was quickly abandoned by residents, and there were no Public Works crews or big equipment assigned to it there, five blocks west. The flow oozed past a fire station, which was also empty, its crews called elsewhere. So flames and molten rock along this street went unchecked.

But at the end of the street, people had gathered outside the First A.M.E. Church. Pastor Lake and his congregants, including Kevin Stock, DeNiece's brother, raced up the block to flag down a squad car—the first they'd seen in some time. It was the squad car of Officers McVie and Jasper, assigned to this area to clear it.

As Pastor Lake came running up, McVie leaned out the driver's window. "You folks should clear out of here," he said. "We're getting everybody out. Flow's headed down here."

"What about the church?" Pastor Lake panted, pointing at it. The church faced straight up the street, right at the flow.

"All the fire companies are engaged right now," McVie said.

"Yeah, saving Beverly Hills," Kevin said, stepping up.

The officers frowned at each other.

"Let's all move along," Officer Jasper said, leaning over in front of McVie. "Okay?"

"Not okay," Kevin said. "Why don't you guys *do* something?"

"What we're doing," McVie said, "is advising you to evacuate right now, before you get burned up."

"We're *already* burned up," Pastor Lake fumed. "*What about our church?*"

"Nothing more we can do, Reverend," Jasper said.

They rolled up their windows and pulled away, hearing shouts and catcalls behind them.

"Baboons," Jasper muttered. "Won't even save themselves."

"Maybe there's something in that firehouse," McVie said.

"Huh?"

"Hoses or something."

"And do what?"

"Maybe try and help."

"It's not our dance, partner. We got our orders."

"I know, but—" He braked to a stop. "Look there." McVie pointed to a hydrant beside the car. "It's not a block away from the church."

"So?"

"Let's give it a shot."

"What shot?"

"If we could find a hose, you got a hydrant right here—"

"Lemme ask you: if this here was *your* block

about to go up, you think one of these bozos would pick up a hose for you?"

"Ain't the question. It's about what *we* oughta do."

"Bullshit."

"Then you take off. I gotta give it a shot." He opened his door.

"You're so frigging naive. They're gonna hate you no matter what."

"It ain't about love."

"You're nuts."

McVie got out. "Tell the lieutenant I'm off my noggin. And tell him you know where to find me."

As Officer Jasper drove off, McVie trotted back to where Pastor Lake and Kevin were trudging back toward the church, and he grabbed Kevin's arm. "You're gonna help me."

"Me!" He pulled his arm away. "Help you what?"

"Let's go." He started back the other direction, toward the firehouse.

"You ordering me?"

"I'm *begging* you."

Kevin shrugged, got an affirming glance from Pastor Lake, and took off at a trot with McVie.

South of Wilshire, on Fairfax, where the main lava flow, minus the offshoots that had slipped south from Wilshire on cross steets east of Fairfax, was still gobbling up parked cars and machines and storefronts with its two-thousand-degree appetite, it was a war zone. Firemen continued to pour water on its front, managing to cool small segments—vainly, because these darkened segments were quickly overrun by more and more lava. Dozens of cars, or, more precisely, burned-out, warped hulks, were now being carried along. Odd bits of steel or pipe or indefinable things ducked up here and there, and disappeared just as quickly.

The noise was pandemonium—sirens, alarms, lava bombs, shouts, and the clanks of heavy machinery melted into the hiss of the lava itself. The populace that hadn't already fled was fleeing now. Cops and others struggled to get the Public Works loaders and tractors in front of the flow—sheer futility given that with a few exceptions they were untrained and unfamiliar with how to operate this heavy equipment. Machines ran into each other or into buildings; a front-loader driven by a security guard did slow pirouettes in the middle of the street. The few that were manageable were engaged in digging up the street, pushing anything possible in the way of the flow. Drivers, only some in hard hats, ducked their heads from the heat, glancing up to find their way.

Just beyond this turmoil of men and

machines, separated only by them from the ferocious lava, was the Rock of Ages convalescent home, a two-story hive now as the elderly patients were assisted, rolled, carried out of the doomed structure into the snowfall of ash by cops and others wearing—those who could find them—surgical masks. Some of the patients were oblivious, some were enjoying the action, some were terrified and in tears. As the lava streamed west on Wilshire, the stream of patients scurried north and south.

A few paces from that exodus, near a Unocal gas station, Fire Captain Heck Reed raged at Public Works Supervisor Roger Lapher.

"You gotta get me some pressure! The hydrants are dry!"

"I got a whole city to worry about, Reed!"

"A city burns one hydrant at a time, goddammit! It's gonna start right here! And you're gonna be the blame, Loafer!"

Not far from them, his free hand plugging his ear from the diatribe, Roark rasped into the cell phone, his voice already showing strain. "Kaiser's no good. It's south of us. All the patients have to go to Cedars . . . it's the best option we got left. Beverly Center is using its own power. They're gonna do triage there . . . What?"

What had happened was that down in the OEC bunker Chief Sindelar had grabbed Emmit Reese's headset away, and slapped it on his own head. "Listen, Roark, I'm getting all the reports I need on hospitals. We need *coordination* with your department. This is the sorta thing you could be head-manning yourself, *if you were here!*"

"I'm trying to get in there, Chief."

"Bullturds, Roark. We sent Gator out after you. I'm dealing with problems I hired *you* to deal with."

"Nobody hired anybody to deal with *these* problems, Chief. A downtown *volcano*. You got no idea. But the K-Rails are on the way, and as soon as they're down for a barricade, and the corridor we're planning is working, I'm outta here. Promise."

"Promises ain't worth fairy spit, Roark. Nothing personal, but you already broke a few, and another one ain't no great comfort. You gotta *be* here."

"Ten-four, Chief."

Roark tucked the phone into his pocket, and, with highway man Levy and LAPD Lieutenant Fox, and trailed by a couple of TV cameramen whom he had managed to ignore so far, set off down Fairfax to approach again the front of the lava war, toward the area near the Unocal station, where a US Geological Survey van was parked. Everybody had ash, like dandruff, on their heads and shoulders.

As they hustled along, one cameraman directly behind Fox chatted to a cohort: "So I said, 'Honey, you talked me into missing OJ's Bronco chase. I'm not missing *this*.' And she says—"

"Scram!" Lieutenant Fox spun around, his hands clenched. "You deadbeats can go suck your thumbs someplace else! Get outta my face, or you're gonna have a couple of busted snouts! Then you can sue me, and I'd love it!"

The TV people slowed down and pouted, let some space develop between them and their quarry, knowing that they could gradually wheedle their way up close again. Just because this was lava instead of a serial killing didn't mean they couldn't do their jobs.

At the Unocal station, Lapher and Reed continued their standoff: ". . . Water! Whole city needs . . . One neighborhood at a time! Can't just stop everything so you can . . ."

Over the din of the scene came the rumble of four flatbed trucks rolling east on Olympic toward Fairfax. The trucks were piled high with pieces of concrete—three-foot-tall K-Rail highway dividers. And behind the four trucks carrying those came four more, each bearing a wheeled crane.

Levy beamed a smile and clapped. Roark and Fox lightened a bit, but remained rather stone-faced.

"Now we're getting somewhere," Lieutenant Fox grumbled.

"Let's get 'em off," Roark said.

As the truck noise grew to dominate the block,

Amy Barnes stepped out of the back of the USGS van. Her grim expression didn't change as she began to maneuver through the throng of firemen, cops, rescuers, and reporters toward Roark.

"Okay," Roark said to Levy, striding toward the trucks now idling near the Unocal station, "I wanna start the corridor here. Keep everything on Fairfax, off the residential streets. When're the rest of them getting here?"

Levy looked like he had been punched in the belly. "Um, this is it," he said softly. "All of them."

"What are you talking about?"

"Um, we were lucky to get this many. Everything else is in Riverside County or stuck on Five, where there was an overpass break."

Lieutenant Fox took a step toward Levy, but was restrained by Roark's arm.

"Easy, Lieutenant," Roark said, not taking his eyes off Levy. "What've we got here?"

"Eighty, twenty per truck."

"Eighty ain't gonna do it."

Levy shrugged. "Well–"

"Can we chopper more in?" Fox asked, controlling himself.

"I'm not—"

"No way," Roark interrupted. "Ash is too thick." He waved his arm skyward.

"They ought to be able to fly in that," Levy said.

"No, this isn't normal ash. These are rock bits. These in the intakes will knock 'em out. Gotta think." Roark was so tired he couldn't think. He found himself being almost resigned.

"How 'bout I knock down a couple *buildings* to corral this sonofabitch?" Lieutenant Fox offered, with a hoarse chuckle.

Roark rubbed his forehead. Abruptly he headed over for Lapher and Reed.

". . . Quake took out the power in *Canada*," Lapher moaned, "and we're supposed to chip in—"

"We got a couple streets melting!" Reed spouted. "Nobody gives a shit about Canada! Vegas ain't out!"

"I'm busting my ass, and all I get—"

"Knock this shit off!" Roark barked, striding up. They fell silent, looking at the ground. "What is *with* you people? We got a crisis, you sound like a couple of spoiled brats. Just listen up! Captain Reed, how long before this flow reaches Olympic?"

"Well, it's been varying speed, depending on how much water we can put on it. And now we aren't getting cooperation on our hydrants and—"

"Give me a *time*!"

"Maybe fifteen minutes, give or take. It's chewing up blocks quicker now, flows a little heavier."

"Is that enough time to build a barricade?"

"What kind of barricade?"

"Like this." Roark pulled a street map out of his back pocket and a pen out of his shirt and on the back of the map he sketched as Reed craned his neck to see. "It's like a horseshoe, a cul-de-sac. Eighty K-Rails double-stacked. That's a wall six feet tall."

Lieutenant Fox had joined them and looked over Roark's shoulder as he drew. "What makes you think it'll hold, Mike?"

"Why not?" Roark looked up.

"That lava is heavy shit, just keeps coming. Everything it doesn't eat it pushes away."

"Well, maybe it'll hold. We gotta try *something*."

"Why don't you drop a bomb?" Lapher offered. "Something like that? Blow that sucker to smithereens."

"Jesus, Lapher, this ain't a pile of dung. We've got endless lava here, pouring out, mowing down everything in front of it, hot enough to melt Alaska. It already *is* a bomb."

"It'll collapse the street," came Amy's voice. Their heads whipped around. "You pool that much lava, all those concrete barricades, on streets with tunnels and tubes and sewers under them, they'll collapse."

Roark stared at her for a moment. "Okay," he nodded, "good. The deeper the hole, the more we can trap. Right here." He jabbed his finger down toward the asphalt.

"Jeez, I don't know," Lieutenant Fox said. "We could go down with it. Or it could pile up and explode. Who knows what could happen, you start damming this stuff up."

"The gas station's indefensible," Roark said

evenly. "And everything south of us is residential. You got an alternative?"

"Such as?"

"I'm asking *you*, Lieutenant. Or any of the rest of you. Don't just tell me you're worried. Give me a better idea." He looked around at the group, everybody looked away. "Let's build a wall, Lieutenant."

11
IRRESISTIBLE FORCE

Cranes maneuvered around the flatbed trucks, unloading the K-Rail concrete dividers. Hard-hat crews with thick gloves attached cables, signaled to lift, and directed the crane drivers where to lower the rails. LAPD cars, emergency vans, and fire trucks converged on the scene, along with other heavy equipment. Parked cars were pushed rudely aside, demolished in the process. The rails were treated like precious, privileged saviors—which is what they were meant to be.

Roark directed the operation, squatting over his crude map, hollering instructions, pointing out positions.

Amy knelt next to him. "What's next, Roark, filling sandbags?"

"You got anything positive to say?"

"A lot of dedicated people are being put at risk," she said, more gently, "by staying around here to do this. I don't see how it can work. That's all."

"It has to. Call me Mike, okay? That'd make me feel better."

"I know three Mikes. I'm used to Roark. You got more important things to worry about."

He felt stung. But when he looked over, she was smiling.

"I'm on your side, Mike Roark."

Red Line #4 train was literally a shell of its former self—the insides burned-out, the entire lower portion melted. Lava had flowed under the entire length of the train and now emerged beneath the rear compartment, just where the members of the rescue crew had two minutes before departed with the unconscious victims slung over their shoulders.

All members except Stan Olber, lugging Hector Solis. Olber was staggering through the last compartment, not from the weight but from the heat. He came to the door and looked down. The track bed was covered with reeking, bright orange lava. It extended three feet beyond the train, and with every moment he gazed at it, it was inches farther.

"Jump!"

Pete's voice caused him to raise his head. Pete had come back after depositing his load, and was ten feet away—as close as he could come. "Jump, Stan!"

"Get out of here!" Olber shifted the load that was Hector Solis on his shoulder, trying to retain his balance.

"You can't save him; just leave him and jump!" Pete beckoned to him.

But Olber wasn't about to leave this unconscious driver behind, not after he had dragged him out of the cab and carried him all the way back through the train.

The lava inched on, lengthening the distance. Olber tried to dip his knees and spring.

But it was not so much a jump as a stumble. Olber landed in the lava. He screamed in a way he couldn't recognize. Nor could he hear Pete's scream. He staggered forward two steps without feet as he hoisted the body off his shoulder. And as he fell forward he heaved with whatever force he had left.

Hector Solis landed just beyond the reach of the lava, and was quickly dragged away a few more feet by Pete. Olber fell facedown in the lava, and when Pete looked up again, there was no Olber at all.

*   *   *

A dozen parishioners knelt in prayer with Pastor Lake on the sidewalk near a fire hydrant, where Officer McVie stood with a fire hose over his shoulder and a big hydrant wrench in his hands. They faced in the direction of the lava flow, which was moving toward them fifty yards away. Fifty yards behind them was their First A.M.E. Church.

"Back to the church, everybody, move it!" McVie ordered.

Pastor Lake rose and motioned everybody to follow him. Rather than turn toward the church, though, they all took their steps backward, their eyes on the lava.

McVie attached the hose to the hydrant and clamped the wrench on the valve and opened it up. The hose filled, writhing like a snake, and stiffened. He dragged the nozzle to the church, where Kevin Stock was waiting as instructed.

"You grab ahold of the hose behind me," McVie said, "and help me hold it steady."

"I ain't no fireman," Kevin said.

"Me neither. Let's pretend."

The lava widened in front of them.

"Now!" McVie pulled back the nozzle lever, the hose bucked, the stream hit the lava. A giant hiss and a cloud of churning steam came at them. The front of the lava darkened, cooled, slowed. But a renewed flow slid forward underneath, a fiery blob big as ever. It was now twenty yards away, hissing, steaming, and coming.

"Lord have mercy!" Pastor Lake intoned.

"We ain't stopping this with no firewater," Kevin grunted.

"Yes we are, yes we are." McVie fanned the nozzle back and forth to direct the stream across the front. "Just hold it steady."

The parishioners huddled behind Pastor Lake, who leaned back and raised his arms heavenward. "Lord, I know you don't like to do it here, but maybe just today you could rain a little on our humble church!"

Out on Little Santa Monica, Hok Duk Kim stood nervously behind the locked door of his 7-Eleven convenience store, staring intimately through the glass at a large crowd of people almost nose to nose with him, some of them pounding on the windows, raising fists, demanding entry.

Hok Duk Kim held his shotgun so tight that his knuckles were white. "Not riot!" he bellowed. "Not all people! I let in one at a time!"

At the counter, his wife crouched behind the cash register and spoke soothingly to him in Korean.

He nodded. "This lava-free zone!" he called out. "Evybody can buy here. But owny one at a time!"

An Arrowhead Water truck pulled into the lot, loaded with bottles of spring water behind its locked panels. Before the wide-eyed driver could put the truck into reverse, the crowd turned away from Hok Duk Kim and surrounded the truck.

The driver cracked the window. "Twenty bucks a bottle!"

People started waving twenty-dollar bills.

Twenty yards from the A.M.E. church, the lava lapped over the curb and consumed the signpost advertising Pastor Lake's next sermon: "Why Sin Seems Fun." The plastic letters melted and popped, the wood crackled. McVie and Kevin aimed the hose here and there, but it seemed to have less and less effect.

Pastor Lake and the parishioners had retreated up the church steps, but McVie wildly waved them away, off the steps, to the side; the lava was aimed right at the church. McVie and Kevin kept hosing it down, the lava kept coming, they kept backing up.

Soon they were on the steps.

"We gotta split!" Kevin shouted.

"You go. I can handle it from here."

"It don't look like you got it exactly under control."

"Jesus, it's hot!"

They were back up against the church doors.

"Get out of here, Kevin!"

"I don't hear you!"

Off to the side of the church, the parishioners clasped hands together, swaying and howling in prayer. Pastor Lake paced back and forth in front of them, wringing his hands, glancing about as if looking for something he had lost.

Kevin kicked back, kicked the church doors open. The lava lapped up the steps. They backed into the church, directing the stream now down right in front of them; the water flashed back in their faces as steam.

Pastor Lake suddenly dashed away, returned moments later pulling the end of a garden hose from which was dribbling some water. Some of the white planks around the double doors were now burning. He went as close as he could tolerate and tried to sprinkle water from the hose on the wood. Two parishioners, shielding their faces with their arms, ran up and grabbed him and pulled him away.

The entire facade was now in flames. McVie and Kevin were inside. The flames were now sizzling the fire hose itself.

The six-foot-tall horseshoe barricade of double-stacked K-Rails was almost complete, installed right in front of the Unocal gas station at Olympic and Fairfax. Lieutenant Fox was galloping everywhere, directing crews and machinery: cops, National Guard troops, Cal-Trans employees, firemen—all of whom were hustling like ants. There wasn't a minute to lose, because the main flow of the debris-laden lava had now crossed San Vicente at Fairfax—a block away.

Roark was watching the progress, fidgeting, pacing, keeping one eye on the lava, the other on the hustling crews. It was all he could do to keep from jumping in and directing everything himself. But this was Fox's job.

"Mike Roark."

He turned to see Amy leaving the USGS van, hurrying toward him.

"Hey, Amy, anything—"

"There's lava in the Red Line."

"What do you mean, 'in'?"

"We just got the word on CB emergency, from people in the hole. It ate a subway train. Lava's spreading through the tunnel."

"Jesus. Everybody okay? Everybody get out?"

"Everybody but one. Stan Olber. He rescued the driver, the last on the train. He got caught."

Roark was speechless, frozen, for a moment. Then he said, "Lava, in the tunnel. Must have got down a manhole or something from the street."

"I don't think so. I think it's coming from the magma chamber. I think it's a major flow. And I think that means there's lots more down there, under us."

"But there's no way to know, right? Could be just a little tributary, like a leak."

"I crunched the numbers, Roark. The volume of this flow up top isn't what it ought to be. I've been curious about it from the beginning. It just isn't enough."

"The guys fighting this thing at the front might disagree with you."

"They've never seen a volcano before. I have. Hot spots are popping up too many places. This stuff is heating a wider area than can be explained by what we see on Wilshire and Fairfax."

"But it came right out of the Tar Pits."

"We're eight miles west of MacArthur Park, where the lake was actually *boiling* last time I looked. So there's a primary heat source right under there. That heat source is lava. How'd the lava get to the Tar Pits if it wasn't moving laterally, *underground*?"

"Yesterday you said it moves straight up."

"Just like it flows down through gravity. But whether being forced up by pressure or drawn down a gravity path on the surface, it takes the path of least resistance. We've never tracked it under a *city* before. We've never had a chance to see what it'd do if it had man-made tunnels to go through."

"But there's tunnels everyplace—subways, power, water, sewers . . ."

"You got it."

Amy started away, toward an unoccupied Fire Department car.

"Where are you going?"

"I'd rather go looking for *it* than wait for it to come looking for us."

Roark's chin sank to his chest as he contemplated this latest evidence, and weariness gripped his eyes. He was too tired to argue with Amy, much less stop her, wherever she was going.

"But you've got to tell me *something*," Professor Heim pleaded.

"That's all we know, sir. She and Dr. Barnes left in the van to investigate some heat anomalies. That was a couple of hours ago. We haven't heard anything since."

"Nothing?"

"Just a minute, please."

He waited for a full minute. He waited two full minutes. Finally she came back on. But her manner was totally different.

"I'm sorry. We've received some unsettling. . . . I'm afraid there's nothing I can tell you right now."

She hung up.

Farther to the northwest on San Vicente Boulevard, in relative safety since the flow had bent south, Third Street was blocked off from traffic, and the area outside the Beverly Center, a couple of blocks from Cedars-Sinai, was being used as an open-air triage center. Victims carpeted the street, stretcher to stretcher, blanket to blanket, body to body. Ambulances continually arrived with more—not even bothering to use their sirens now.

The Hard Rock Café was being used as a holding area for uninjured people who couldn't get home. There were Red Cross representatives doing what they could to calm them down, and waiters were serving free snacks and soft drinks.

In a corner, Kelly sat on a chair with her bandaged leg extended, talking to two small boys.

"I'm Chuckie," the slightly taller one said. "I'm five. This is my little brother, Tommy. He's four. You have to keep an eye on him, Mom always says."

"Okay. You know the game Rock-Scissors-Paper?"

"Yeah," Chuckie said. Both boys held out fists.

"Okay. So rock beats scissors. Scissors beats paper."

"I'm lava," Tommy said. "What beats that?"

"My dad," answered Kelly. "I hope."

Lava already surged against the completed, man-made, horseshoe-shaped barricade constructed of stacked concrete highway dividers. Fifteen fire trucks nosed in behind the K-Rails, nuzzling them for added support. Firefighters manned hoses and water guns on the trucks.

Captain Reed addressed the men through a bullhorn: "Not a drop until I give the word!"

The lava, which first nipped at the base maybe six inches deep, now rose, inching up along the concrete. The barricade groaned with slight, imperceptible shifts.

High up in his unfurnished Beverly Tower penthouse, Norman Calder surveyed the scene through binoculars: ash floating down on fires, exploding lava bombs, wild car crashes, maneuvering of heavy equipment, scurrying medics. The noise of all that didn't reach him. He heard Chopin piano on the stereo he'd had installed.

He reached for a cordless phone and punched in a number, holding the binoculars to his eyes with his other hand. Through the north windows, he could actually look down on the block-long triage area.

Jaye Calder didn't answer the phone by herself. She had her hands in a scrub bowl on an outside table on Third Street, surrounded by victims, washing up for another medical procedure. A nurse held a cell phone to her ear. "Yes?" she said impatiently.

"You wouldn't believe what this city looks like,

with all that's going on, from twenty stories up," her husband Norman said.

"I really can't talk now, Norman."

"You really shouldn't be down there now, Jaye. I want you up here, where it's safe."

"There are people *suffering* down here, darling," she said with a degree of incredulity. "More patients than we can handle. Surely you understand."

"No, I don't. From up here, I can see things you can't. This damn thing is spreading, darling. People are going crazy. It's all out of control. You're endangering your own life."

"Norman—"

"I've been watching. You guys are dealing with open wounds. You're not wearing gloves or masks. Who knows what these people are coughing up on you? Could be AIDS, anything."

"Coughing?"

"Well, smoke inhalation and all that. You deny people are coughing?"

"I don't deny anything, Norman. I gotta go."

"I demand that you come upstairs."

"Later, darling." She moved her head away from the phone and nodded to the nurse that she was finished.

Those watching the lava against the barricades were now oblivious to everything else. Firefighters, emergency crews, Levy, Fox, Roark, all of them watched silently as the lava pooled against the concrete and inched up it, almost as if mysteriously seeking the gas station that lay beyond.

A bead of lava found a seam between the rails and appeared on the back side of the barricade.

"Lieutenant!" hollered a patrolman, noticing it.

"Yeah," Lieutenant Fox gritted his teeth. "This stuff is beginning to frost my ass." He scampered back to the gas station and returned with a bucket of water, which he angrily tossed on the rivulet of lava. That slowed the intrusion, but didn't stop it.

"Keep doing that," he said to the patrolman, tossing him the bucket.

Down in the Red Line tunnel, the lava had finished feasting on the #4 train. Only the top half of the cars remained, charred black. But then the flow had slowed and finally stopped. Lava lay cooling across the tracks. A safe hundred yards up the tunnel, MTA engineers with flashlights checked the integrity of tunnel walls for leaks, while on the station platform Fire Department medics treated the former passengers for smoke inhalation.

Amy entered the station unnoticed by the harried crews, climbed down to the tracks, and proceeded west from the ruined train, down the dark tunnel into its still-unfinished section. She shined her halogen flashlight ahead of her into the gloom, looking for a sign she hoped she'd recognize of a presence she wished she wouldn't find but knew was there. It was there, somewhere, ahead of her.

She would have preferred not to be alone in this excursion. But it was too important, too urgent, to stop and haggle about it, or worry about somebody beside her who would be too afraid to continue. Rachel would have joined her, and been perfect for it. But there was no Rachel. It had already taken Rachel. Perhaps it would take her. But it would have to show itself first.

12
BREAKTHROUGH

The lava rose, hissing against the barricades, heaving its collected pieces of junk against the concrete where it scraped upward.

"It's gonna go over," Lieutenant Fox said.

"Maybe." Roark shifted his feet anxiously.

They all stood off to the side, away from the horseshoe. All eyes were on the rising lava. Breathing was short. The enormous pressure against the stacked dividers was causing them to creak and shift. One fire truck, then another of those nosed into the horseshoe was moved backward an inch or so by the force and weight of the sizzling molten rock.

"I'm sure it's going over," Lieutenant Fox said, as the lava reached the top.

"Maybe. Jesus. I don't believe it. What's holding the street up?"

Lava began to drip over the top, onto the hoods of fire trucks, where it instantly burned holes in the steel right through to the engine blocks. Roark closed his eyes.

Then there was a new cracking sound. The pavement groaned and buckled. An explosive rumble came from within the horseshoe, shaking the ground under the vehicles and crews, and suddenly it collapsed.

The pavement under the lava fell, taking the orange lava with it, ten feet below the surface of the street, where the whole mess fell in a tumble of sparks, smoke, flame.

"Now!" Captain Reed bellowed. "Hit it!"

A dozen fire crews opened up at once, directing the streams from their hoses and truck-mounted guns into the hole. Enormous clouds of white steam shot up. Lava continued to push forward and spill into the huge sinkhole that had been created by the collapse, taking everything within the loop of the horseshoe except the barricades themselves; the pavement under them held.

There were some isolated cheers from the crews. Everything was going right for the first time since the volcano had opened up in the Tar Pits. And added to the success, just as magically, was that as the sinkhole predictably began to fill up with lava, the flow seemed to diminish. It became obvious. The flow over the lip of the sinkhole became much shallower, the pace slower.

The mood became suddenly hopeful. A few men raised gloved fists even as they continued to pour water onto the deepening pool. Lieutenant Fox flashed a brief smile.

But Roark did not smile. The very thing that caused everybody else to cheer—the diminishing flow of lava—disturbed him. What Amy had said, the logic of it, had stuck in his mind. He wondered. Was this success something to worry about?

Stained-glass windows crashed to the floor, leaded shepherds melted and burned. The facade of the First A.M.E. Church was burned away, exposing, until they too were gone in the flames that engulfed them, studs and Sheetrock.

Tear-stained faces of the prayerful parishioners reflected the yellow flames. Pastor Lake was on his knees, not in prayer but in mournful defeat. The struggle to maintain and sustain this church through the years had involved threats and intimidation and human violence; through the years this parish had withstood desertions and diminished interest and smaller wallets, and even two smaller fires—maybe arson, maybe not—that ruined in one case the altar and in another seven pews. Pastor Lake had gone without salary when necessary, had preached tough tolerance and gentle forgiveness through thick and thin. Sometimes he had longed to be transported to a nicer place, a heaven on earth, or even, during a rare mood of despair, a heaven in heaven.

But who in heaven's name could stand up to this eruption from the guts of the earth itself?

"Lord," he said quietly, in a desperately weak moment as the irresistible flames seared his church, "I truly believe I've done wrong in this life. But I've not done *this much* wrong. You're doing more wrong to me and my folks than I ever did to You. You'll forgive me for speaking so openly."

McVie and Kevin backed a few steps farther into the church. Through the flames they saw a vehicle wheel up beside the lava on the church lawn and skid to a stop.

"You see that?" Kevin sputtered through lips dripping with sweat and swollen from heat.

"Yeah. Bastard Jasper's back."

It was Officer Jasper. He sprang from the driver's seat and raced to the back and flung open the back doors. The van was loaded with fire extinguishers. He began tossing them to parishioners. "Just do it!" he yelled.

They did, charging at the church as a brigade, directing their feeble sprays at the spreading blaze.

McVie chuckled meanly through a hoarse throat. "Stupid bastards. . . ."

But he and Kevin kept doggedly hosing down the lava, barely able to see.

It was imperceptible at first, then more apparent: the lava was slowing down, the front of it cooling under the hoses. McVie charged it with the nozzle, watching it thicken and stop. And the fire extinguishers were in fact dousing the flames on the flimsy exterior wood, saving the main frame.

"What the hell . . ." Kevin muttered, blinking to see through his sweat.

"I don't believe it," McVie said, stepping now right on the cooled rock surface of the lava to move the hose forward.

Outside, Pastor Lake dropped his empty extinguisher and sank again to his knees. "Thank you, Lord. Uh, nothing personal, Lord, on that other. Anybody can get confused, a time like this. . . ."

Amy stopped, feeling her heart thump, and shined her light forward. Instead of the beam penetrating down the tube, suddenly the tunnel seemed to end right in front of her. She was confronted by a wall of dirt and debris. She examined it more closely. It wasn't flat. It wasn't the end of the tunnel, either. It had caved in from the side.

"Oh my god," she mumbled, stumbling backwards.

She turned and ran, tripping over ties, back toward the MacArthur Park station.

The flow on Fairfax had totally stopped. The lava hardened where it lay, creating a solid mirrored black surface over the rest of the still-molten rock. Firefighters still trained their hoses on the sinkhole, but it was not rising anymore.

Gradually it dawned on everybody, and shouts rang out, cheers. Men whipped off their helmets and high-fived each other, patted backs.

"Did we just beat this bastard?" Lieutenant Fox asked.

"Maybe," Roark answered.

At last the sun could be seen rising above the horizon. Truly morning. Everything brightened beyond the hazy dawn that had muddied the scene like a too-small lightbulb.

Workers paraded over to congratulate Roark. He shook hands, acknowledged praise, thanked them back. He began to believe it himself.

His phone jangled. He took it out of his pocket. "Roark."

"Amy Barnes."

"Good timing. We've finally—"

"We got a problem."

"Not anymore. I'm trying to tell you we've stopped the—"

"Big trouble. How fast can you get to the corner of Wilshire and Western?"

"Soon as I can find—"

"Listen. I think that eruption up there may be just a vent."

"A vent?"

"Not the main exit. And the vent on Wilshire could just be clogged—wall rock could do that."

"Meaning?"

"Let's assume that we haven't seen the bulk of the magma yet."

"Jesus. That's what you think?"

"I'm waiting. Hurry."

A boy Kelly's age was sitting next to her as she played with the two smaller boys.

"This isn't so bad," he said. "Maybe it'll blow out my school."

"There are a lot of people hurt," Kelly said.

"Yeah, but I mean, other than that." He brightened. "You wanna see Pearl Jam's platinum album? They have it hanging in the back."

"Jeez, yeah. Now, Chuckie and Tommy, you guys

stay here for a minute, okay? Right here. Until I get back. Promise?"

"We promise," Chuckie said.

Ten minutes later Roark was roaring toward Western Avenue on an LAPD Harley-Davidson that he'd found lying on a curb. He wondered what could be so wrong—Western lay back to the east of the worst part of the problem. What could be going on there?

Amy was pacing in front of a sign that said, in big red Gothic letters on a white background, "Future Red Line Station." It was a construction site, surrounded by a chain-link fence.

"Come on," she said, with no other greeting.

Inside the fence was a huge excavation, a massive pit, with a dirt ramp descending perhaps two hundred feet. Around the hole were several dump trucks and flatbeds.

"Come on," she repeated, charging ahead of him.

They descended quickly down the steep dirt incline—clearly a ramp for trucks to get in and out. At the bottom, they walked through the underground construction site toward a dark unfinished tunnel that extended in either direction.

"Okay," Roark said, as they passed a trailer office, a crane, a nest of jackhammers, piles of cables and ropes, a big pallet on which lay scores of green compressed-gas tanks, "what's going on?"

"This tunnel collapsed about two miles east of here."

"Maybe they just aren't finished digging."

"No, it collapsed. The composition of the earth, the way it's piled, the angles. Yadayadayada. Trust me, it collapsed."

"Could have been the quake itself."

"This was pushed in from the side. It's *bulged* in."

The only light they had was Amy's halogen. She didn't hesitate at the entry. They walked quickly into the tunnel, headed east.

"None of this whole disaster makes any sense, does it?" Roark said. "A volcano under Los Angeles. Christ."

"Every seismic zone in the world has volcanoes. California has forty. Why *wouldn't* there be one here? Cities are no more than zits on the face of the earth, hardly a deterrent to magma."

"Yeah, but a *city*—"

"You ever hear of Pompeii?"

"Yeah, but modern day. No city is more modern day than this. I mean, up-to-date and upscale and high-tech. Plus, I just figured that we got earthquakes, mud slides, forest fires, loony politicians, losing sports teams—the Great Spirit ought to cut us some slack."

"All the natural stuff hangs together, you know. Volcanic mountains, cycles of fire and rain and wind. It's all part of the grand cyclic scheme. Magma from the mantle pushes the mountains up, like the San Gabriels. Rain and snow flows into the San Gabriels. They erode, and what they're made of pours down, and we have the slope to the sea. The plates push against each other, magma pushes up, new mountains are created. Volcanoes make new crust with stuff from the middle. All cyclic. Everything that happens up here is affected by what happens down there, in the mantle. We don't take the Great Spirit's hint: people shouldn't have built a city here in the first place."

"Well, it's a little late to worry about that."

"Yeah, it's a little late."

"But see, that's what makes engineering so exciting. The hurdles. Solving problems, overcoming difficulties, that's the whole point. That's why I'm here. Every week we've got another crisis, and every week we answer back. It's inspiring."

"It's arrogant."

"Come on—"

"Nothing personal. I agree that solving problems is exciting and inspirational. But I prefer to face problems that *we* don't create. There's enough to do. Like, here we are on such a volatile piece of crust—why would anybody put a subway under this city?"

"Same reason that. . . Whoa!"

They came around a bend, and four hundred yards straight down the tunnel was a massive face of lava, almost filling the tunnel with glowing orange magma steadily advancing.

Roark stared. It was the biggest flow yet.

She walked a few steps farther. "It's actually kind of beautiful, don't you think?"

"Are you *nuts*?"

"I mean, as an absolutely pure natural force."

Roark was panting. "It's bigger than Fairfax, bigger than Wilshire."

"It may be the mama of it all. The mama magma."

"Let's get out of here!"

"Think first, Roark, before you run. This isn't a museum exhibit. This is the real deal. So we have to *deal* with it. This flow will move through this tunnel until something stops it—and something will, eventually, because the tunnel's not finished, so it's gotta run into the end. Then it'll build pressure and push where the resistance is least—it'll bust through the surface, like it did at the Tar Pits."

"Oh Jesus."

"Where'd they stop tunneling the Red Line?"

"The Beverly Center! Cedars!"

"We might have an hour. That's enough time to evacuate."

"They've got bodies wall to wall there, Amy. And we can't get choppers in or out."

"We've gotta get them out. And we gotta deal with the lava flow. That's all there is to it."

The lava had advanced a hundred yards as they watched it.

"My daughter, Kelly—"

"Let's go."

They trotted back to the construction site in the open pit. Roark reached into his pocket for his cell phone. Then he stopped.

"Goddammit."

"What?"

"Shine your light around the site. There! That's acetylene in those tanks. Welder's gas. They're bad as the volcano. They'll blow, and when they do they'll take the whole block out."

"You're right. You got any ideas?"

"Can you drive a truck?"

"Try me."

A few minutes later she was partway up the ramp behind the wheel of a Kenworth flatbed, used to haul bulldozers, cranking the starter.

Roark was twenty feet below her, using ropes to rig the pallet of acetylene tanks together and attaching the pallet to a chain from the hook on the rear of the flatbed. The lava was just emerging from the tunnel onto the construction site—a ten-foot-thick flow.

"Come on!" he hollered.

She ground the starter. Nothing.

"You're flooding it!"

She leaned out and hollered back. "Shut the hell up, Roark!"

"Come on!"

"*You* wanna try, you ape?"

He checked the rigging, and, glancing back at

the tall lava face spreading across the floor, scrambled up the slope to the truck. An explosion on the floor caused him to whirl around: the first vehicle the lava reached, a little Bobcat loader, had blown up.

The flatbed started. Roark jumped onto the running board. "Go!"

Amy carefully accelerated, feeling the chain behind her tighten. The truck stalled.

"You flooded it."

"A woman always floods it, right?"

"Sorry."

"Hold on." She tried the starter, gently pressing the accelerator. Again. It caught. She let the clutch out slowly. The chain was taut. The pallet gradually began to move—just ahead of the lava. The truck wheezed up the incline until the pallet was clear. She stopped. They turned to watch.

The relentless lava wave rolled across the dirt floor of the future station, majestic and powerful in its color and force, absorbing everything it contacted.

"Whew!" Roark exhaled.

"You gotta control yourself, man. We had it all the way."

They shared a small laugh, watching the lava flow below the pallet.

But then they stiffened. One of the tanks had fallen off and was rolling down the ramp.

Roark yanked her head down just as the tank hit

the lava and blew. The concussion rocked the truck and smashed the rear window. Pieces of rocks covered the dashboard.

Roark peeked up. The other tanks stayed on the pallet.

They looked at each other, this time with no laughter at all.

Amy's hair blew wild on the back of the police motorcycle as Roark darted around obstructions and abandoned cars, headed back to the main war zone.

He was on the radio to LAPD Chief Sindelar, still at the OEC bunker.

"It's bigger than the one on Fairfax, Chief. Incredible. Forget the others, this is the real threat."

"We'll move the patients as fast as we can, as far north as we can get 'em. We'll commandeer everything we can find."

"There're too many. We're gonna have to attack the flow. Find a way to block it or divert it somehow. Focus everything on it."

"Roark, the damn thing's everywhere."

"What do you mean?"

"*Everywhere*. Fairfax has buckled all the way down to Venice. It was lava shit, in a storm drain under the street. Took out the Genessee transformer. The whole Westside's dark."

"Where's that flow now?"

"Dumping itself into Ballona Creek."

"*What*! Wait!" The bike swerved, almost went over. Roark pulled over to the curb and stopped. "What'd you say?"

"It found Ballona Creek."

"Chief! Ballona Creek runs to the ocean—right through Culver City to Playa Del Rey!"

"Yeah. We caught a break on that one."

"But don't you see? Listen. There's a guy named Porter, Public Works, supervising the Hollyhills trench project. I need him at San Vicente and Third Street in five minutes."

"How'm I gonna find him?"

"*Find* him. He's around. I also need a demolitions team, *loaded*."

"What're you driving at?"

"I'll be there in five. Out."

He cranked up the bike.

"So what *are* you driving at, Roark?" Amy asked.

"You'll figure it out."

Kelly returned from a rear section of the restaurant carrying a tray with two hamburgers, french fries, and diet Cokes. As soon as she spotted Chuckie, she called, "Food!"

Then she stopped. "Where's Tommy?"

"He went through there," Chuckie said, pointing

back toward the kitchen. "He said he was going with you."

"Oh-oh."

"Can I have his fries?"

"You wait here or I'll beat the tar out of you."

Kelly limped back the way she had come, toward the kitchen.

Roark could see it. It lit up in his mind like the magic-lantern shows his parents used to have when he was a little kid in St. Louis—among his earliest memories. It was as clear as that, a panorama. When he saw something like that, he never forgot it—it was indelible.

What he saw in his mind was the trench outside his house, the hole covered with steel plates. That ten-foot-deep trench was gouged all the way up his neighborhood of Crescent Heights. It veered at San Vicente, still headed more or less north. Up San Vicente a few hundred yards the trench was open, no metal plates. There the trench ended. Beyond that was half a mile of unbroken asphalt, all the way across La Cienega to the intersection of San Vicente and Third.

Back at the beginning of this route, running the other direction, was the dry concrete bed of Ballona Creek.

That was the picture.

Right in the middle of the far end of that picture, at the intersection of San Vicente and Third, not far from Cedars-Sinai and the Beverly Center, in the very shadow of Norman Calder's splendid new twenty-story Beverly Tower that dominated the corner, Roark spread an MTA subway map on the hood of a pickup and indicated his thinking to a group around him: Porter, Lieutenant Fox, Captain Reed, Gator, and Amy.

"Okay. This is the Red Line." He traced with his finger. "It ends right here, under this intersection." He jabbed his index finger down. "Right here." He gestured toward the sign on the intersection sidewalk that announced optimistically:

FUTURE STOP OF THE METRO RED LINE!

It was a pensive group that took it in, amid the diminishing ash and sirens and sense of urgency. They were tired, not fully disposed to Roark's new insight that reached them in the terse summons to be at this place in five minutes. Just a short while ago they were flushed with success, about to be able to relax. Now this. Roark wasn't finished with his presentation.

He unrolled a clear plastic grid map and laid it over the MTA map. The overlay showed the Hollyhills trench—the route that had lit up Roark's mind—going north on Crescent Heights, onto San Vicente, almost reaching the very spot on which they stood.

"This is the Hollyhills storm-drain excavation," he said, tracing with his finger, "connecting to the trench on San Vicente. Now, see the pattern. Anything that gets into that trench is gonna flow eventually all the way into Ballona Creek, here."

"And then to the Pacific," Gator said, the first to recognize it. "Nice."

"And then what?" Porter said, dubiously.

"Let the ocean take care of it. That's the least of our problems. We've got fifty-five minutes to—"

"Fifty," Amy interjected, looking at her watch.

". . . fifty minutes to extend the trench a half mile, up San Vicente to this intersection."

They gaped.

"Extend the trench?" Porter shook his head. "It takes months to do that. We've been working up on Hollyhills for—"

"Not today. We're pulling out the stops."

A panel truck arrived, on its side the identification, "LAPD—Explosives." A sturdy, somber man in blue LAPD coveralls got out and approached the group, giving Lieutenant Fox a quick salute.

"Okay, Armstrong," Fox said, "you're right on time so far."

"Yessir. What's up?"

"You're standing on ground zero. Lava's gonna break through right under us. We gotta reroute it."

"We're good to go, sir."

"Go where?" Porter put in.

"With *you*," Roark said, rolling up his maps. "You're going to show them where to place the charges."

"Where?"

"Under the street."

Porter was jolted a step back. "In the *sewer*?"

"We're going to blow us a trench."

"But, but, we can't—"

"Can it, Porter!" Lieutenant Fox snapped. "As in, we *can*!"

"But, but—"

Roark put a hand on his shoulder and looked into his eyes and nodded. Then he turned to Gator. "Any gas mains or power lines under San Vicente have to be pinched off. That's you, Gator."

"Done," Gator said, turning immediately to leave.

"Captain Reed," Roark continued. "Every patient has to be moved north, above Beverly. That means out of the hospital and out of the street. Big job."

"Consider it under way. We've got the flatbeds that brought in the heavy equipment."

"Wait a minute," Amy said. Eyes turned toward her. "The street slopes the wrong way, right toward the patients. That lava's going to *erupt*. It's likely going to come straight up through the asphalt, and it's not going to go uphill looking for a trench."

Roark closed his eyes briefly, then opened them to scan the area, anxiously focussing finally on the restaurant where Kelly was. Gator strode into his vision, alone.

"Where is she?" Roark asked.

"I don't know. Couldn't find her. She wasn't in the Hard Rock, boss. I've got orderlies watching for her."

Roark closed his eyes again, desperately trying to concentrate on the job at hand.

"They'll find her, boss. Just that there's a lot of turmoil up there. But she's not gonna wander, not on that gimpy leg."

"We're going to build a dam," Roark said suddenly.

There was a silence as the questioning eyes focused on him.

Then Lieutenant Fox said, "A dam. What with?"

Roark looked around at their faces, and said calmly, "Lieutenant, you mentioned it before, about knocking a building down."

"I said that? I was *joking*, for chrissake!"

"That's okay. It gave me the idea."

"What building do you . . . oh no!"

Roark was gesturing with an open hand, like an offering, toward Norman Calder's sleek Beverly Tower. Heads tilted back, and eyes looked up at the structure.

"No . . . no . . . no . . ." were the muttered echoes.

"It was a *joke*," Fox pleaded.

"It's okay, Lieutenant. Nobody's gonna blame you for it. It's a joke that became a good idea."

"But the *Tower*—"

"It's not occupied yet. Look around here. There's nothing else we can put in its way."

Fox mused for a minute. "You want the thing laid down straight, right along the street." Roark nodded. "That's a precision drop, Roark. Takes days to set up that sorta thing."

"You got talent in your department, ex-military sappers, along with your demolitions guys."

"Yeah, but—"

"Think about all those patients. We sent them over here for safety. Now they're not safe here anymore. My daughter's one of them."

"We'll get your daughter out, Roark."

"Don't miss the point. I just want you to know how determined I am."

"And maybe crazy."

"If we do it right, we can steer the flow into the trench. Can't we, Amy?" He turned to her.

She thought. "Theoretically."

"We got something better than theories?" She was silent. "And is there anything other than the ocean that's gonna put this thing out?"

"No."

"Okay, Lieutenant. Put your teams out."

Officer Armstrong looked at Roark, then at Lieutenant Fox, as Fox pondered.

"Okay," Fox said at last. "Split the team. You know the personnel. Put 'em out, turn 'em loose."

"Yessir." Armstrong saluted and trotted back to his truck.

Porter was stalking around in the small circle, shaking his head. "You're not gonna blow up a street and knock down a building. Not in fifty minutes, you're not."

"No, we're gonna do it in forty-five." Roark stopped him with his hand and turned him so that they were face-to-face. "Get aboard, Porter! We know you got doubts! We *all* got doubts! Probably this won't work, okay? But we got our asses to the wall! Let's go to work!"

Porter, chastised, looked away, then back at Roark. He nodded grimly.

"What can I do?" Amy asked.

"Find my little girl."

13
LAYING THE CHARGES

While this quiet planning was going on, the city was fleeing. Freeways were jammed. Radios and television blared doom. Word was out across the land. The federal government was mobilizing forces, air drops of men and matériel were being planned a continent away. The Army Corps of Engineers was poring over topographical maps of the area. The US Geological Survey was licking its chops over all the data it would amass. People all over the country were glued to the news. The whole idea was incomprehensible. Yet the news was sparse, on this first morning of lava being loose in L.A. Not many reporters and cameras were able to penetrate the action—not because they were barred by officialdom, but because physically there was no easy way to get into action central. If this lasted a couple of days, the public all over would be awash in pictures and interviews and expert analysis of tectonic plates and volcanic hot spots and the grand scheme of the earth's crust, magma, and core; there would be plenty of grim assessments of how Los Angeles didn't belong where it was.

But all this was happening now, in just one day. By tomorrow and the day after that, the scope of the havoc would be known; the volcano would be established. What happened today would determine what was left of the city.

Unseen and unheard in this last hour was the advance of the lava under the city, through the Red Line subway tunnel. The mighty river, with its horrendous heat and force, was muscling its way west. While plans might be made about it, it was under nobody's command or control. Wherever it went underground, the surface above got hot. Wandering cats and dogs yowled and hopped dizzily away, having stepped onto sizzling asphalt. Streets sagged.

From wherever the magma was gathered in a chamber deep in the crust, the pressures continued to send it up. There was more and more. For a while it was contained in the tunnel. But nothing could contain it under the streets for long. It would make an exit for itself. That would be soon.

The lava reached the end of the tunnel and started to pool.

The mass exodus was under way at the outdoor triage area on San Vicente, and at the Beverly Center and its environs. Wheelchairs were pushed, stretchers carried. Hundreds of volunteers joined the effort. The flow of damaged refugees headed north, to the area above Beverly Boulevard.

"Move it, move it!" Captain Reed commanded, striding through the melee. "Every patient moves!"

Dr. Jaye Calder, her head fuddled with exhaustion, pushed a gurney up the street. Her husband Norman leaned in with a hand to help.

"I *knew* that damn subway was bad news," Norman said. "Of course, I thought it'd mainly bring us drug dealers and gang members—lava didn't occur to me. But I *told* you it was bad news."

"I heard you, Norman. It doesn't matter now."

"But we need to learn a *lesson* from all this. It's been a tremendous waste."

"Norman?"

"Yes, darling?"

"Put a cork in it."

In the Hard Rock Café, people were being led out through the doors. Against this exit flow, Amy elbowed her way in.

"Kelly?" she called. "Kelly? Kelly?" The light was

not good, and she was dazed from the work and worry, so she knew that finding her would not be easy. But this was where she had to start.

Kelly had been in there until moments ago, when she had limped off to find four-year-old Tommy. She walked through the now empty kitchen, calling, "Tommy? Tommy?" She went through a door into a vacant service corridor and downstairs and into one of the access tunnels beneath the Beverly Center.

She caught a glimpse of a small figure disappearing around a corner ahead. "Tommy?" She tried to run.

Officer Armstrong led his team of five down into the stinking sewer line under San Vicente. Each man was laden on chest, back, and waist with sticks and sacks of explosives. With Armstrong was the Public Works man Porter, color drained from his face, his eyes round as a salmon's.

"Double-time, men," Armstrong directed.

They picked up the pace, huffing in the hot confines.

*   *   *

In the basement of Norman Calder's tower, Sergeant Hap Riley led the other team of five out of a stairwell into the garage.

"Hey, Hap," one of the demo team called. "I forgot to rub your head for luck!"

"You got all the luck you're gonna get, white boy," Riley answered, chuckling. "If you're *really* lucky, you got all the luck you're gonna *need*."

"Think we can pull this off, Hap, for real?" asked another.

"Never been anything I couldn't blow up," Sergeant Riley said. "We'll be okay. Every one of you knows how to do this."

"You ever think about an afterlife?"

"I been too busy with this one. Come on, down here's what holds this damn building up, where we gonna bring it down."

"What about this car?" a patrolman asked, indicating a blue Jaguar.

"Forget about the car," Riley said. "Its owner must be long gone. Say good-bye."

Over south Beverly Hills, a police helicopter circled low, its loudspeaker booming a message:

"This is an emergency. Clear the area. Your life is in danger. Clear the area. . . ."

Below the chopper, in Mrs. Gooch's Market, most of the shelves were already empty. Residents and servants had started hitting these shelves with the first shocks of the earthquake and hadn't quit. Now just a few things were left.

"I hear the Valley is safe," said a woman in a maid's smock wheeling a cart at top speed through an aisle.

"Why's this sort of thing have to happen *here*?" moaned another woman, in a Gore-Tex warm-up suit. "We've done everything possible to keep this neighborhood safe."

"Well, some things you can't buy," said the maid. "Including no more milk."

"We're all packed to go, but we can't find our cat, Muffin."

"Better forget Muffin, lady. She's probably running north with the rest of us. Everybody's all alike now, 'cluding cats."

The triage center was now on Beverly Boulevard. Patients filled the street and kept flowing in.

Jaye Calder made what in more normal circumstances might be called "rounds," checking each gurney, stretcher, blanket, and wheelchair.

Norman paced right behind her. "You've done your duty, Jaye. Can't we leave now?"

Jaye felt spacey. She could barely feel her fingers as she placed her stethoscope on one chest, then another. Her own heart thumped. Her feet hurt.

She had to force her eyes to focus to check supplies on IV lines. ". . . Can we go . . ." she heard.

"Norman, you still here? Sorry, what did you say?"

"I said, can't we go now? You can barely stand up. You've done all you can."

"No, these people—"

"They're *strangers*, Jaye. I mean, other people can take care of them. You don't have to *die* for them."

"I'm not dying." She picked up a wrist to check a pulse. "I'm just tired. You go ahead. I'll be along."

"Jaye! You're half-asleep. Do you know what you're saying?"

She turned to face him. "Yeah, I do. I can't leave. You go. You're in my way."

"I can't believe you're saying this."

"Please. Take care of yourself."

"You're not a saint!"

She turned away, back to the patients. "I'm a doctor."

Not far away from the Calders, Roark hurried among the patients, checking faces.

"I can't find her!" he said frantically.

"You will," Amy said behind him.

"What if I don't?" He turned and looked past her, scanning the room.

"Where could she go? Even if she's not here, she's safe somewhere."

"I should never have let her be taken away."

"Stop it," Amy said. She put a hand to his cheek. "Just stop it."

Armstrong's men were having trouble keeping their footing in the sewer under San Vicente. They were having trouble holding on to tools. Sweat poured off them and slickened everything as they laid their explosive charges.

"Easy, easy . . ." Armstrong cautioned his men. "This stuff ain't Silly Putty."

They moved fifty yards up the pipeline and knelt again to place the explosives. Then fifty yards more. The stench made the men queasy, but none of them complained.

Porter fell to his knees and retched onto the pipe. The busy men laying the charges ignored him. "Can I get out of here now?" Porter asked.

"We're almost finished," Armstrong said. "Hear the pounding upstairs?" He hooked a thumb at the ceiling of the sewer. "That's the guys busting up the street."

Above ground, on San Vicente east of La Cienega, earthmovers and loaders and jackhammers attacked the asphalt. Gator reported progress into a cell phone.

"Yeah, we're moving," he said. "But I'm telling you, it sure seems like a long way to go."

"We got fifteen minutes," Roark said.

In the basement of Beverly Tower, Riley's squad attached plastic explosives to the north-facing pillars.

"Come on, come on!" Riley pushed his men. "We got twelve minutes. And I mean, I'm gonna blow this in twelve minutes! Ross, leave that, it's good enough!"

"It's not very neat, Hap."

"Forget neat, it'll do it. Let's get the detonating cord run."

Norman Calder stepped out of the stairwell, heading for his Jaguar. When he saw the men crouched around the pillars, he walked over. "Uh, can I help you fellas?"

"This is a restricted area," Riley said, looking up at him, looking him over. "You better get out of here."

"This is my building. I own it."

"Oh, well, you better get out of here. It's coming down."

"What?"

Just then the ground began to shake. The Jag's alarm began to wail. The men scrambled to secure the explosives. Norman stumbled to his knees.

Everybody looked up at the ceiling, hugging their gear.

"Let's go!" Riley shouted. The man scampered for the stairwell. Riley followed him, dusting his knees as he went, and the others brought up the rear.

Then Norman stopped and turned back. He ran instead for his Jag.

The squad raced up the stairs, hearing the roar of Norman's Jag coming to life.

In the sewer line, the shaking was even more violent.

"Everybody out!" Armstrong ordered, wondering if the walls of the pipe would hold.

Porter headed for the manhole first, but the shaking buffeted him aside just as he was reaching the ladder, and the side of the ladder caught his cheek and slit it open. Another man helped him up. Porter was sweating so hard that the blood that dripped off his chin and ran down his chest was as dilute as pink lemonade.

The men followed Porter out of the manhole, Gator reaching down to pull up each one. He got three up, four.

Not far down the road, a piece of asphalt shot into the air.

*   *   *

At the intersection of Third and Vicente, the pavement started to cave in. Along with the rumble underfoot, windows were crashing all around.

"Everybody, off the street!" Lieutenant Fox yelled to his patrolmen stationed around the critical spot. "Let's scram. She's coming up!"

The asphalt was cracking and beginning to heave. The intersection bulged.

And suddenly a huge explosion blasted the neighborhood, and a geyser of lava flung rocks into the air. A column of lava ten feet wide shot up two hundred feet.

The last man to come up the manhole ladder was Armstrong. Gator reached for him just as the explosion hit. Armstrong fell backwards, his head clanging off the rungs until he thudded at the bottom.

Gator grabbed the phone at his feet. "Do not detonate! We've got a man down in the sewer!"

He dropped the phone and slid down the ladder.

Calder roared out of the garage, onto the street, then screeched sideways as lava blocked his path and began immediately to flow around the car. Riley's men sprinted out of the building, and Calder leaped from the car and raced after them. They were only a few steps ahead of the flowing lava. Ash was covering everything, and everything was burning. The street was flooded with lava that was expanding faster than a man could run.

At the triage center outside the Beverly Center, Roark yelled into the phone: "Lieutenant, you gotta detonate! You gotta pull the trigger now!"

"One of my men is down! One of yours, too!"

"Oh Christ!" He knew it must be Gator—the only one of his own men accompanying the sappers.

From his vantage point, Roark had witnessed the geyser of lava and rock, and now saw that the lava was already heading toward them. For a moment he was hypnotized by the scene.

Into his intense gaze came something else: somebody walked out of the Beverly Center garage, a little boy, as casually as a Sunday stroll in the park.

"Wait!" Roark yelled into his radio. "There's a kid there! Hold it!"

As explosions continued marching up the street toward his view, he saw Kelly emerge.

"Hold it!" he railed vainly against the din. "Stop the explosions!"

He dropped the radio and ran.

"*Kelly! Kellleeeyy!*"

He sprinted down San Vicente, right into the teeth of the lava.

On the other side of the eruption, Gator emerged

from the manhole, painfully dragging up Officer Armstrong behind him. He grabbed the phone from the street, hoisted the unconscious officer over his shoulder, and began slogging away.

"Fox! We're clear! Blow it!"

It was an amazing and eerie tableaux for an instant. Gator trudging away to the south, where they'd been laying the charges under the street, carrying the man he had saved; on the other side of the eruption, the side of the Tower, Lieutenant Fox fielding the message and about to raise his hand to signal the blast they'd set up; and up the street, behind Fox, was Tommy, and a ways behind him, Kelly, walking with slow stiffness, and behind her Roark, running pell-mell right into the middle of what would blow.

"Detonate!" Fox cried, swinging his arm down.

The bottom of Calder's Beverly Tower bulged and blew, dirt and glass and steel exploding outward.

From beneath the street, five explosions went off sequentially, each blasting rock and asphalt into the air. At La Cienega, San Vicente gave way totally, exploding into the sky.

The explosions marched along Gator's trail, and the fifth caught him and threw both him and Armstrong into the air like rag dolls.

*   *   *

Calder's building began to creak and groan and lean. Standing right beneath it on San Vicente, Kelly, her eyes glazed, covered her ears from the horrendous noise that surrounded her. The building was starting to fall, in the slow-motion way that huge towering things seem to fall.

Roark leaped over a finger of lava, shielding his face from the heat with his arm, his trousers, and the soles of his shoes, smoking. Still he registered the looks of terror and disorientation on the faces of the two children as the world disintegrated around them.

He leaped for the two of them just as Kelly reached Tommy, hurling them forward.

The building crashed down in a mushroom cloud of dust, sending out a concussive roar that echoed even amid the volcanic din. It fell right on the line Roark had asked for and the engineers had designed and the sappers had arranged. Lava moving northwest slid against the massive pile of rubble, veered, and slid along it—to the southeast, following the line of the building. It followed the building to the new-blown trench, twenty feet deep and twenty wide, opened by the explosives placed by Armstrong's men. The trench began to fill with glowing red-orange magma from the center of the earth. It slid down the trench. Encountering a newly broken main, it turned the spouting water instantly to steam, not slowing in the effort.

The lava flowed down the trench, past the bodies of Gator and Officer Armstrong. Thunder added to the rumble. Rain began to fall.

Amy walked along the back side of the fallen building, stepping through the rubble that separated her from the lava. She had seen Kelly approach this spot, then Roark. Now they lay under the building. Her wet hair hung straggly down her cheeks. The rain became heavier, breaking through the cloud of ash. She walked on.

Roark appeared from around what had once been the top of the building—the penthouse—cradling Tommy, leading Kelly by the hand. They stumbled through the wreckage toward Amy.

"We made it," he said.

"Yes," Amy said. "Jesus, yes you did."

Suddenly they were laughing.

The lava filled the trench entirely, twenty feet deep. It slid down San Vicente all the way to the Hollyhills trench, into which it spilled and disappeared under the steel plates. It moved on under the plates, turning them red-hot one by one as it passed, making them sag and finally fall. It slid past the Roark house. It slid beneath Venice Boulevard, then spilled into Ballona Creek, which turned it toward the sea.

The lava slid for miles on this strange path, through Culver City, under Slauson Avenue and Culver Boulevard, down through Playa Del Rey.

There it met the sea. It oozed into the Pacific hissing and screaming, sending up great gouts of steam and spray, where it gradually slowed and hardened into shapes like giant pillows, piled deeper and deeper as the lava continued to pour in from behind.

The lava entering the Pacific left a continuing trail of itself all the way back to the geyser that continued to spout at the intersection of San Vicente Boulevard and Third Street in West Hollywood.

The geyser was only a fraction of its original height now, just about ten feet, but the lava from it continued to flow into the trench and creek and head to the Pacific. Everything in the vicinity was covered with a layer of ash, everything and everybody.

Professor Heim touched Amy's arm. She turned around. "You're Dr. Barnes."

"Yes?"

"I admire your work. You were Rachel Wise's boss."

"Yes."

"Tell me what happened. Please. I didn't know her very well, but . . ."

Norman Calder dusted off his hair and shoulders as he walked through the broken glass and chunks of concrete and twisted pieces of steel that used to be his building. He paused beside LAPD officers Bud McVie and Terry Jasper, who were watching soberly as two bodies were carried away. Then he moved on toward where medics and doctors were working on patients, new and old.

"Jaye," he said, finding his wife working as before. "You still speaking to me?"

She looked at him, unsmiling.

"I'm so sorry, I—"

"I need a nurse over here!" she called, bending back over her patient.

He stepped back and turned away, continued his walk.

Lieutenant Fox sat on the curb, Tommy on his lap. Fox's men had located his mother and radioed that they'd be bringing her in.

Roark sat beside Kelly, holding her tight to him, her head nestled against his chest. She dozed on and off. "That worked a little better than I thought it would, Lieutenant," Roark said.

"Yeah. But it worked. I guess it worked."

"Reports have it tracked all the way to the Pacific. It worked. There's no sign of anything new to surprise us."

Amy walked up and sat down beside them. They all looked at the geyser, whose power was still diminishing.

"She okay?" Amy asked.

"She will be. Just the burn. It's not so bad. You okay?"

She nodded. The rain was beginning again, and she closed her eyes and turned her face up into it, loving the cool rinse. "You were right, you know. You thought this thing could be fought. And you were right."

"*You* were right, Amy. We got lucky."

"Anyway, you couldn't have done better."

"We couldn't have. No."

A black-and-white squad car stopped in front of them. Chief Sindelar got out from the driver's side, Emmit Reese from the other. They looked around, awed by the destruction, the lava, the geyser.

"Hey, Mike. You find Gator?"

"They found him."

Reese studied Roark's stone face, understood it. "He didn't make it."

Roark looked at the ground and shook his head.

Reese turned away, folded his arms, watched the erupting lava.

"I hope you got a couple bright ideas left, Mike," Chief Sindelar said.

"Oh yeah?"

"We've got flooding all over Beverly Hills. The water mains busted, you know. Mud slides in Malibu."

"Yeah. Find somebody else." Roark rose, stretched, stooped to scoop up Kelly, and walked away toward where Jaye Calder was treating the wounded.

After a moment, Amy rose and followed.

*   *   *

The volcanoes didn't last long. The one on San Vicente ceased erupting two days after it began. The original at the La Brea Tar Pits poured out a flow for another month, then gradually pooped out.

Ten months after that, Los Angeles had returned to stride. Golfers approaching the sixth hole at the Wilshire Country Club had to chip over a strand of shiny black obsidian—lava that had cooled too fast to crystallize. A place called "Volcano Burger" did a thriving business at what used to be a traffic intersection—Fairfax and Olympic—which was now a field of glassy lava. What was planned at the Red Line stop on Western was no longer a tube, but was filled solid with cold black lava. Norman Calder's new twenty-story "Lava Tower" was set for occupancy soon. San Vicente Boulevard was now just a street of slick hardened lava, with yellow lines painted on it to form traffic lanes. Ballona Creek was just a long black rock.

On a warm fall day a year after the volcanic eruption, Mike Roark and Amy Barnes sat on a bench holding hands and gazing at the dark two-hundred-foot cone that loomed right where the Tar Pits used to be. An occasional wisp of white smoke rose innocently from the crater.

"What are you thinking?" Roark asked.

"We're still here."

"That's it?"

"Hey, that's a lot. Think of it, Mike. We're still here, looking at that thing."

"And it's still here."

"Yeah. It'll be here long after we're gone."